WESTFALIA

WESTFALIA

Blake Hill

Bolt Press

Bolt Publishing

11150 W Olympic Blvd, Suite 750
Los Angeles, CA 90064

Copyright © 2021 by Blake Hill
ISBN-13: 978-0-9827351-1-4

Library of Congress Control Number: 2021903691

Editor: Bonnie Hearn Hill
Cover design: Dominic Forbes
Motorcycle logo: May Samari
Typesetting & book design: Bradley Miskell

First Bolt Publishing printing: March 2021
First Bolt Publishing Hardcover printing: March 2021

Visit byblakehill.com

Printed in the United States of America

CONTENTS

for my kids

dream

can i dream at 52
can we live as we do
our lives imploded with a hug
she said undo with a shrug

i am 52

twenty five years with only one
one for me and now i'm done
one for her and she's through
we lost sight and away she flew

i am 53

my days went dark as months ran
my soul bled from within, bye bye little clan
what i thought, what i knew, just blew
my shades of black slowly glide to blue

i am 54

can i dream at 54
can i open another door
yes. today is an outstanding day
i am filled with dreams as love guides my way

INTRODUCTION

"Sometimes in life the fog rolls in and you need a compass."

The premise of this book started with a hug. At the time of that embrace, I didn't realize a book was being conceived. She gently pulled me in for the hug and whispered these two words. "I'm done." I was confused by those two words, completely thrown off guard. I ask her what she meant.

"What do you mean you're done?" I asked. "Done with what?" She quietly whispered in my ear, so the kids couldn't hear, "I'm done with us."

My heart sank, and a numbness of emotion consumed my entire body. I couldn't understand how we could be married for twenty years, and now it was over. What about our kids? I grew up in a broken home and made a pact with myself at a young age that I would never get a divorce or put my kids through one. Divorce was not an option for me. But then again, it takes two for a relationship to be a relationship.

I left that summer, flew from Hawaii to British Columbia, and decided to ride my bicycle across parts of Canada. I couldn't get her words out of my head. The hug played over and over. I needed to be in nature and just peddle. I was riding from Banff to Jasper one day and had to cross over a mountain range. The entire day's ride was more than 120 miles, and I had to climb approximately 10,000 feet in elevation. I knew the slow grind of an ascent would do me good. There were no options except put my head down, crank the music, and peddle. As I began to reach the top, ice pellets bounced off my helmet, and my super thin jacket did nothing for me. I didn't care. The moment felt rewarding and appropriate. I'm no stranger to bad weather. I've been caught in blizzards while riding my motorcycle across Montana, New York, and other places. All I could think was, bring it on. I really don't give a fuck. It was on that climb that this book came to me. Here I am in my fifties, with two kids, and soon to be divorced. I knew there was a lifetime of emotions bottled up inside, and the divorce was the catalyst for their release.

I waited sixteen months before starting the book. I had to live through the emotions that would exude from my soul. Yeah, there were some long days and sleepless nights. Most nights I really didn't want to goto bed because I didn't want to wake up to a new day. There really weren't new days though. They all felt used, dirty, and embarrassing. I did it though. I went to war with my emotional self for sixteen months. On the sixteenth month. I had accepted divorce, but I hadn't forgiven my wife. That thought was my catharsis.

I stood at the base of the mountains behind my house with my two dogs by my side and offered my forgiveness to my wife. That moment of clarity made me realize I had to forgive her in order to feel whole again. I wanted happiness in my life. I wanted love in my life. I knew that I had to lead by example and show my kids by my own actions.

The gut-wrenching blow of any life-changing experience is truly a time to reach deep within yourself and find out who you truly are and allow that person to come through so you can experience happiness, peace, joy, and love. When you're a parent, you have to role model that for your kids because one day they could be walking in your shoes.

The story you're about to embark on is a dream that takes you on a spiritual adventure filled with past, present, and future experiences.

Life is truly an adventure when you let go and live it.

Let the dream begin.

Love life, Live life...

"The cave you fear to enter holds the treasure you seek"
Joseph Campbell

1

DENIAL

"Denial is the blind eye to fear"

I'm done. I can't drive another mile. My head feels like a brick. The hum in my ears has lost its comforting feeling. My ass is so numb I can't tell if I peed my pants or if I'm sitting in sweat. I really don't know what to feel. Are feelings even appropriate?

I stand outside the van encapsulated by huge trees. A starlit night sky with no moon. Damn, it's dark. I reach into the side panel of my door and find my headlamp. All I can think is-Where's the moon? I can't stop asking myself and I'm actually starting to annoy myself. Where's the moon? Where's the moon? It's so frickin' dark, and I have no idea where I've driven. At this juncture, I really don't care, and it really doesn't matter. My life is a blur, a trainwreck, and I'm housing a brick for a brain. I fumble around in the dark, reach up to scratch my head, and realize, oh. I have a headlamp on. What a putz I am. It's so damn dark that the beam of the light resembles a high-powered spotlight. The van glows in the beam of the light. Yes! I can see my priorities were straight when I packed. Not sure I would actually call it packing. More like stuffing a bunch of shit in a van in under two minutes. The only two things that matter are the surfboards strapped on my rack. A slight sense of relief creeps into my soul, but that is short lived when I relive the hug.

It wasn't an ordinary hug, but is any hug ordinary? It is meant to spread goodness, right? Shouldn't we always feel emotion when we give or receive a hug? And who is considered the receiver of a hug? So, if someone came to me and asked, "Do you want a hug?" Are they asking for a hug? Are they asking if we can both hug? Am I giving or receiving? Yes. I would love a hug. I let out a huge sigh of frustration. Well, the hug I received was filled with emptiness, loneliness; it was cold, angry and bitter. I was hugged by a rock, and when I tried to hug the rock back, my soul was instantly filled with deep, dark shards of pain. I tried to deny them. I ignored them, but the pain was trying hard to penetrate my presence along with the ice-cold words she muttered.

Perhaps, I once again didn't fully listen. I was good at not listening or hearing what I wanted to hear. After twenty-five years, you do hit auto-pilot occasionally. If I defined occasionally with a percentage, that number feels like my IQ at the moment. Is it 50 percent? Is it 75 percent? I know I can drop the number to 10 percent. I'm happy to go through life with a low IQ. I try to tell her this, but she's not taking the bait. I'm staring into her eyes; can't find a soul, or perhaps I'm blind too. Maybe it's a reflection of my soul. I don't know. I seem to be talking and can't hear my words. All I feel is the cold, hard hug of steel.

I run the scene over and over and over. Why didn't you say

the right thing, you idiot? I'm actually trying to figure out what I did wrong. I look to the stars as if an answer will fall from the sky, and life will be normal again. Hey God. I'm here. Send me a note. Feel free to use the sky as an Etch A Sketch. I'm so frickin' dumb, numb, and desperate that nothing makes sense. In a flash, my life has turned to shit. I want to scream, but nothing is coming out. Would a scream zap my energy? Do I need to scream, or do I need to sleep? I need something. I'm so damn lost that I need energy to guide my ass to bed.

I've popped the top on this camper van a thousand times, but tonight, it's as if my fingers are broken. The van houses a lifetime of shared memories, and right now, I want to hit the delete button and forget everything. The top popped, and I lumbered to bed. My body had residual vibration from the drive, my legs tingled, my elbows ached, my fingers cramped from hours of squeezing the wheel with a death grip. I felt at least one hundred years old. I wiggle my toes and stretch my legs to the end of the bunk. I'm tall, so I really don't fit. My body lies diagonally, so I can almost squeeze my body in the bunk. The pillow has that familiar smell of camping; mildew, campfire, and dust. I don't care. It's comforting. It's familiar. I think a piece of my soul lives in here, and at one time, two souls lived in here. I'm looking for gratitude, but it's too damn dark. I try to meditate, fuck that. I can't find my soul. The only mantra I hear is her voice on a loop. I want a divorce. I want a divorce. I want a divorce. I want a divorce. I want a divorce. I want a divorce.

"Turn it off," I shout. "Turn it the fuck off! Who quits after twenty-five years? I was a good husband. I never stepped out of the marriage, even when your ass got plump and bouncy."

I was always front and center for the kids. I didn't drink. I didn't do drugs. I'm thinking maybe I should have. I went surfing, rode motorcycles, and drank coffee. Come on, I took a motorcycle ride once a month with the guys, and she puts me out to the curb like a piece of garbage. It's Monday morning, time to put West out at the curb. I've been fired. Wow! I've been fired from some really shitty jobs but to be fired by my wife. It's absolutely mind-blowing.

Oh crap, I just realized I didn't brush my teeth. Does it really matter? I doubt I packed my toothbrush. Fuck it. Who cares? I'm sleeping by myself. Crap! Now I have to pee. I'm not doing it. I'm not getting out of bed. I'm exhausted. I'm beat. My eyes are twitching like fleas on a dog. I need help! I'm asking for help. Please. I'm asking the universe, god, anybody who can hear me.

Sleeping in the van brings comfort and love. Not sure I really feel the love but the sense memory of comfort overwhelms me. Exhaustion had taken its toll. I was out. I could feel my body tingling and twitching as I allowed myself to go under the spell of three Ambien. The directions said take one. I don't know: three felt like the magic number. Typically, I like to do everything in even numbers, so three felt appropriate. I'm a big guy who wanted to turn the chatter off. I was drowning in chatter. I wanted quiet. The same story kept playing on loop. I wanted peace. I wanted the illusion that the hug never happened. You can't end twenty-five years of marriage with a hug. I was convinced we could work it out. We always had. We made a pact from day one to never use the D word.

Divorce. Shit, we've been through harder times than this. A couple of therapy sessions, and life would be normal again. I repeated this to myself over and over and over. Life is good. I faded away.

My dream was so peaceful and light. It felt more real than a dream. I was sitting on my surfboard waiting for a wave, surrounded by friends. We were laughing and making jokes. I turned to look at the beach as the golden morning sun sprayed through the clouds and lit Dawn's ginger hair on fire and left it glowing. Her beautiful, bright hair sucked me in. I gave a nod with a smile as she held up two cups of coffee, gesturing for me to join her. I turned to look out to the horizon and watched the wave of the day stand up. I turned to catch it and shouted to my buddies that I was going in. The banter of voices erupted, giving me a hard time for going in to my girl. I was going, no matter what.

I popped to me feet and rode the wave all the way to the sand. What a great feeling. There's absolutely no better feeling than catching the wave of the day. I made the drop and pulled a bottom turn that pulled my longboard to the lip. Then, I cross stepped to the nose of the board and rode it all the way to the beach. I'm certain it was the longest nose ride of my life. Joy exuded from my entire body. I was stoked, high on life. My day was complete. Water dripped from my hair and ran down my face. The taste of salt water mixed with the touch of the sun felt like heaven. I licked my lips as though I had eaten the last bite of the world's greatest dessert. The ocean brought me elation, joy, and community. There was no place I'd rather be. I wanted to hold this moment in my mind forever. All I could think was, why would I want anything else? Is this bliss?

I walk to Dawn and place my board in the sand, excitement raging through my body. I can't contain myself as I sit down beside her. She playfully throws a towel at me, and I miss the catch as it engulfs my face. I wipe the water from my eyes and plop to the ground. The smell of coffee is strong and vivid. It's as if I can see the aroma. I mutter thank you as I put my lips to the cup. I feel the warm sensation of caffeine roll across my tongue, and the avalanche of liquid cascades into my gut. Dawn's lips are moving, and her hands are talking for her. All I can hear is the rumble of coffee flowing down my throat. I don't hear a word. I have no idea what she is saying. Her red hair radiates in the golden sun as we lock eye to eye. I'm desperately trying to hear the words rolling off her lips. I'm asking, "What? What are you saying?"

I'm distracted by the corduroy of lines rolling across the ocean. In my head, all I can think is, oh my god. It's waves for days. Everyone is scoring wave after wave. Clean, glassy overhead waves peeled all the way to shore. This day is magical. It is utopia. Did I die and go to heaven? Pure silence consumed my presence as the coffee waterfall froze. A cold chill overtook the warm golden sun. My body felt like ice cubes. I was stiff like an old man. I turned to look at Dawn, but my spine felt like I was rotating steel. The motion was slow and very mechanical. She was gone. I couldn't find her. I couldn't hear her. The image of a man in black and white popped in front of me. He had huge eyes with massive whites showing and a voice like James Earl Jones. And all he said was, "She Said..."

The guy scared the crap out of me. My eyes popped open as I stared into pure blackness.

I'm that person who needs to know the time in the middle of the night. Is it time to get up? It's weird. I don't hear any waves crashing. There has to be something. The forecast called for 3-4. I dig under my pillow and feel around for my watch. Oh, there it is, it's on my wrist. What a goof I am. I laugh at myself. At least I can laugh at my broken ass. What? I look at the time. I've been asleep for thirty minutes. How could that be? I peel my watch from my wrist and toss it across the van. I'm done with the time. Who cares? I try to fall asleep, but my neck itches, my head itches, my entire body itches. What the hell? I want to sleep. That's all I want. I close my eyes and feel my energy surging throughout my entire body. I feel like a refrigerator running. Please god, let me fall asleep. And if you're gonna give me dreams, let me dream about the time I rode a motorcycle with Gandhi. That's a great dream. Maybe I wouldn't be in this position if I would have listened to Gandhi. He's a pretty wise dude, and I could have learned from him. That's it, I'm taking a hand full of Ambien. It's so dark I can't see, and if I turn on a light, I'll be awake forever. I lumber out of the bunk like a giraffe in a chicken coop. Then, I reach and feel for where I think the bottle is located. Oh great. Here it is. I can't see how many I've dumped into my hand, nor do I care. My big hand holds a lot of tablets. I toss them into my mouth without counting. I'm desperate. I want out of my head. Wow. That was a mouthful. I let as many as I can fall under my tongue. I read somewhere that will get them into my bloodstream quicker. It's probably a useless piece of info I've stored in my brain, but hey, I used it. I try to peer out the window, but it's exceptionally dark outside. I crawl into the bunk and pull the pillow tight into my body.

I feel like shit. I feel like a huge failure. I told myself, you are a fucking failure. How could I be the failure? I didn't ask for the divorce. I didn't quit. I'm a great dad and a good husband. I know how to fix a toilet, write a poem, and change diapers. What more could Dawn want from me?

That's all I could think. What more did she want? Marriage has highs and lows. Frick. Life has highs and lows. It's like we're on a roller coaster for our entire life. The broken record kept spinning. What did she expect? My best friend's wife once told me she had no expectation of her husband. I thought that was brilliant. Nothing made sense right now. Absolutely nothing.

The waves were stacking out the back as I peered to the horizon. It was first light, and my body was pulsating as I sat on my board. I couldn't believe how good it was.

This is off the charts. Holy crap. Where is everybody? I dream of days like this. No one out but me, dreams do come true. The silence is broken by the bark of a baby seal who pops to the surface right by my side. I'm caught off guard and scream like a little girl. A familiar voice speaks and literally scares me off my board. It's the black-and-white guy from the beach. He's in color now. He reaches out and touches me and says, "Good morning, West."

I climb back on my board as his eyes lock with mine. The old man's gaze pierces my soul. It's as if he knows everything about me, and the weird part is, he's standing on the water wearing a hat and a red speedo.

"I don't mean any disrespect," I say, "but you know people don't wear banana hammocks anymore."

He laughs with such intensity that the water ripples from the vibration of it.

All I can do is stare at him. What am I supposed to say to a guy standing on the water? I guess I'll ask him his name.

"What's your name?"

"Charlie," he replies.

That seems like a pretty generic name for a guy who can stand on water.

In the distance, I hear a single-engine airplane chugging along. A banner stretches from behind the plane.

"I have a message for you,"

Charlie says. The plane passes in front of me with the banner in plain view. West, you have been terminated as a husband.

Charlie looks at me.

"Isn't your name West?" He asks.

"Yeah, it is. Did you read a last name? I didn't read a last name. There are millions of people named West."

'You're the only West sitting here," Charlie says. "You're the only person I see for miles."

I can't believe I'm having a conversation with a guy in a spee-do, standing on the ocean.

"Why would I be having this conversation with you?" I look Charlie in the eyes because I really don't want to look at his package wrapped in red.

His eyes radiate a deep blue, as if deep from his soul. It is as if he is pulling pure, everlasting energy from the depth of the ocean.

"You know, Charlie don't surf, but Charlie can walk on water."

I want to ignore him so badly. I want him to go away. I don't want to hear his babbling bullshit. This is my time.

"I don't know," I answer. "What I do know is that the waves are really good, and no one is out. You're killing my vibe, Charlie. You're killing my vibe. I came out here to surf, not chit chat about a broken marriage, broken hearts, fired, terminated, or just flat-out being thrown away like a piece of garbage."

"I don't think Dawn considered you a piece of garbage," Charlie says. "She tossed the entire garbage can out."

"Thanks for the clarity," I say. "That makes me feel better about myself."

"I'm here to help." His voice takes on an assuring tone.

"Really?" I say. "It feels to me you're jamming my self esteem straight to the ocean floor."

"You'll see," he says. "I am here to help, like right now. As you surfers like to say, OUTSIDE!" Charlie's voice bellows. I totally didn't expect him to scream like a maniac. I look to the horizon and see a huge set rolling toward us. I look over to see what Charlie is going to do, but he's gone. The wave looks like the Empire State Building barreling across the ocean and headed right for me. Oh Fuck! I fall to the prone position and jam my arms into the ocean. My heart is thumping as I try to paddle toward it. My adrenaline is going through the roof. Oh shit this thing is coming in hot. That frickin' Charlie guy distracted me. I should have ignored him. I'm paddling like there's no tomorrow, but I'm stuck. I'm not going anywhere. The water feels like glue. My arms dig hard into the ocean but I'm not getting any results. I don't want to panic, but I am. I'm in full panic mode. I want out of here before this monster of a wave eats me for breakfast. I scream to myself, paddle paddle, paddle! My world goes silent. The prop of an airplane engine fills my head as my eyes lock onto the banner. The pilot is pointing at the banner.

It reads, You're terminated, West. Shit. The pilot is that Charlie guy.

I flip him off with both fingers and scream, "Screw you! Screw you, Charlie!"

I look back out to see that I'm not getting over this runaway freight train that is barreling for me. I'm so screwed. This thing is growing in size, and I have nowhere to go. Without hesitation, I ditch my board and take my last breath as I watch this giant pitch from the top. It's behemoth lip is headed straight for me.

I dive underwater like there's no tomorrow. I give it everything I've got, but the power of the beast wins. I feel my body being sucked up the face and enjoy my last two seconds before the ultimate beat-down commences. This moment has an element of peace and tranquility and gives the illusion that things will be all right. I've been here before. That's false hope. My head pops out the top for a millisecond as I gasp for my last bit of air.

The sledgehammer of Mother Nature pile drives me straight into the grips of hell. She pounds me like a rag doll in a Pitbull's grasp. I'm being gang raped by water. Water is penetrating every hole in my body as I'm slammed left, right, up, and down. I'm pretty sure I just did ten cartwheels, maybe twenty. It's a little challenging to keep track. The sounds are horrendous, and my ears are ringing from all the pressure. Bam. I hit the sand. The thud feels like I hit silence. And just like that, my pounding comes to an end.

I sit up to find myself surrounded by nothingness. I'm in the middle of a dry lakebed. The sun looks massive as it backlights a rickety old motorhome that is barreling toward me. Dust spews from the tenement on wheels as it jams across the dry lakebed. I wave my arms in desperation as it races right past me. I scream for help as the dust falls on my head and the sun becomes the moon. My world goes completely silent. Then I hear a familiar voice.

"West, you want a ride?"

He's sitting there on the coolest motorcycle I've ever seen and it has a side car.

I'm actually really happy to see him. I feel as if my entire world has been stripped away from me. Here I am alone in the desert, naked and I don't care. I'm not sure if I really don't care or if I've given up. I was just emotionally and physically beaten to the ground. Everything about me felt like it was stripped away, and I had no choice in the matter.

I stood up because it was the only thing I could do.

"Yes, I would like a ride."

Dust fell from my body as If I had been in the desert my entire life.

"Charlie don't surf, but I can twist the throttle." He laughed and tossed me his red damn speedo. "Sorry West, it's all I got."

He had this amazing look with his leather helmet and old ass goggles. The goggles were cool. They were glass set in thick, brown, worn leather. Me on the other hand. I was not one with my surrounding. I stood there wearing my red speedo, leather helmet, and the same goggles. Why did Charlie's look so cool, and mine didn't? Maybe mine came from Wal-Mart or something? His goggles appeared so old you couldn't put an age on them. If goggles could have wisdom, they had it.

I climbed into the side car. What a cool set up. I had never been on a motorcycle with a side car. For such an old-looking bike, it felt space age. I sat back, mesmerized by all the lights on the dash and felt the warmth of the seat. I felt at home. To my surprise, it was cozy. The coziness was soon interrupted by the intercom in my helmet. This old ass helmet had an intercom system?

"Welcome west," Charlie said. Then, he asked me for what felt like the one hundredth time. "Did you know you got fired?"

I put my head into my hands. I couldn't tell if he was trying to be funny, stupid, or just an asshole.

"I just want a ride, man, just a ride."

"How can I give you a ride when you don't know where you're going?"

I couldn't tell if he was a smart ass, so I said, "Drive in a circle then."

"West," he said. "You don't drive a motorcycle; you ride a motorcycle."

"Great. I've learned something tonight."

Charlie muttered, "merely the beginning."

Off we went into the night. We didn't ride in a circle. In fact, this crazy bastard rode hard and fast. He crouched above the seat like a jockey on a racehorse. I'm pretty sure we had one speed, and that was full throttle. I was sick of Charlie asking me about being fired from my marriage. I had to talk loud over the roar of the wind rushing across my face. I screamed, "Charlie!"

"You don't have to shout," he said. "This is one hi-tech machine. I could hear you from a million miles away."

"I never thought of it as being fired." I told him.

"Well, you were. You got canned. Acceptance is the key here, West."

"Accept what?" I asked.

"Accept the fact you're in denial."

"No, I'm not."

"West," he said. "You're in denial about being in denial. You're so deep into the forest you can't see a tree."

Charlie kept the throttle pinned as if we were racing. He was on a mission. The bike felt magical. The night felt magical. I did not feel magical.

"Where are we going?" I ask.

Charlie never let off the throttle.

"I'm getting you out of denial, but we have a small problem."

"What's that?"

"We need gas!"

All I could think was, this dude is like a wizard, and he needs gas. He's not much of a wizard. I actually don't know what a wizard is.

"Look West," he shouted. "There's a gas station." And right in the middle of nowhere, sitting in pure darkness of the desert was a gas station named, Good Grief.

"Is that for real, seriously. It's called Good Grief?"

"Accept what is before you," he said. "The lesson could come in handy later in life."

I'm not sure I really had a choice. Charlie would stop no matter what, and I was merely a passenger in the sidecar.

Charlie glanced over at me.

"West you're in luck. You can stay in denial, or we can fill up with premium and ride into fear."

"How can I deny something I didn't do?" I asked. "I was a great dad. A good husband. I never cheated. I don't drink. I don't do drugs."

"Blah blah blah," Charlie blurted. "Great story West, you're a choir boy. Open the glove box."

I was confused. This entire situation felt confusing. "What, Charlie?" I put my finger on the button to open the glovebox.

"Stop" Charlie said. "I just had a better idea come to me."

I looked up from the dash and into total darkness. The gas station was gone. Did we pass it?

"Charlie, I thought we needed gas. Did you pass it?"

He looked at me as if I were crazy.

"The bike is fueled by the energy of the universe, no gas required."

Charlie was interrupted by the sight of a refrigerator sitting in total darkness under the beam of the full moon. He brought the bike to a stop directly in front of the fridge. A dim red light shined through the clear glass door.

"Open it," he said, and I turned my head sideways a few times, trying to understand why a refrigerator would be in the middle of the desert. Charlie said it again, "Open the door."

I reached out with hesitation and slowly pulled the door open. The icy cold refrigerator air met the warm desert night air. Charlie said, "Grab one."

I asked, "Do you want one?"

"They're not for me," Charlie said. "They're for you." The bottles were lit by a dim red light. The pure white glass bottles have writing on them. The writing is etched into the bottle. I read, FEAR, ANGER, SELF-DESTRUCTION, COURAGE, ACCEPTANCE, FORGIVENESS AND LOVE. Charlie said, "take one." I reach out for the nearest bottle, which was labeled, LOVE. Bam. My hand smashed into a clear piece of glass that is protecting LOVE. I jammed my fingers into the clear protective glass, "shit, that hurt. Is this a joke?"

Charlie says, "No. You read all the labels except, DENIAL."

I was getting frustrated with him.

"Denial. Denial. Denial. That's all you talk about Charlie. Is this all we're going to talk about?"

He gunned the engine, and we sped away from the cooler stocked with emotions. He jumped. Just like that Charlie jumped from the motorcycle.

I sat there all alone, traveling at warp speed. I was speechless, lifeless, and emotionless. It was if I thought the bike would drive itself. In my head, I thought everything would be fine. Yep, I'd sit there and wait for this thing to come to a stop, or maybe Charlie would climb back on. The wind was blowing in my face as I traveled at excessive speeds into the darkness of the unknown.

The moment felt like an eternity, and the unknown began to take its toll.

"Charlie. Charlie," I shouted. "You bastard."

I told myself to do something, but my words were muttered, and my butt felt glued to the seat. My brain felt like it was covered in maple syrup, super thick maple syrup. It was the ultimate spill that oozed all over my emotions. The cleanup felt impossible. My brain was numb. My heart was numb. And my soul? I had no idea where my soul was. I looked within myself for anything that might resemble one and saw a little boy peddling his bike. Hey that's me. He peddled hard into the darkness and disappeared.

I found myself on a bicycle as I glared at the largest mountain I had ever seen. The peak was swallowed by white cumulous clouds with a gold shaft of light shining from above. I couldn't tell if it was shining downward or upward, and I was seduced by the mountain's shadows and curves. In awe, I stood there with the bicycle between my legs and pulled a water bottle from the frame of the bike. The bottle was huge and I wondered how it could even fit on my bike? But I was thirsty and took a really long drink. I held the bottle out in front of me and read the words on it. In bright orange set against the bottle, were the words "Denial Water Co."

The road sign next to me grew from the ground like a tree. In big letters I read, "Climb the mountain, and you will live in love."

I went from feeling like I was alone to looking away from the sign and seeing thousands of people. They were standing along side the road, wearing red. All I could think is, "Why is everyone wearing red?" I clipped my left shoe into the pedal and pushed off with my right leg. I pedaled for about fifty yards. It appeared easy, but the climb was steeper than imagined.

This sweet little old lady was standing on the side of the road cheering for me. She held a card that read, "Go West!"

The old lady was petite, but her presence was huge. I couldn't help but stop as she chanted, "Go West!"

"How do you know my name?" I asked. "Do I know you?"

She pulled her black-framed sunglasses to the end of her nose, and I locked onto her bright, piercing, glossy blue eyes. I'm looking at her, and she's staring straight into my soul.

"No," she replied. "You don't know me. Are you riding up the mountain?"

I pointed to the sign behind me. "The sign back there says if I climb the mountain, my wife will stay with me."

"Are you sure that's what it said?" the old lady asked.

"Absolutely," I answered with one hundred percent certainty. "It wasn't my fault. I didn't ask for the divorce. I was content with our marriage."

The old lady's head turns to the side like a puppy trying to understand.

"Content? You were content?"

"We had a good marriage, life was busy, driving kids to functions, work. I was a hands-on dad. I did a lot."

The old lady kept nodding her head. I couldn't tell if she agreed or disagreed. I'm thinking she has the answer; for god sakes, she's old. Old people always have an answer. So, I kept talking.

"I never cheated. I was faithful. I didn't do drugs or drink. My life was devoted to my kids. How could she just quit?"

Then the old lady asked me, "Maybe you quit?"

"Me?" I said. "I didn't quit. I might have ignored her. I might have tuned her out. That shit happens after twenty-five years. I didn't quit!" I kept talking, couldn't stop talking. "Why would she quit? Who up and quits a marriage after twenty years? Who does that? What about our kids?"

The old lady reached out with her arm and patted my shoulder. It's crazy, but all I could think was her skin was silky smooth. It reminded me of a baby's skin.

"I'm giving you some advice," she said. I couldn't stop staring at her skin. I was amazed, listening but not really. I wonder if her whole body is that smooth? She does have a few lines on her face. I'm really trying to listen to her advice. She says, "If you stop and tell your story to everyone along the road, you'll never make it to the top of the mountain." I looked down at her cool red Converse tennies.

"I love your shoes."

I clipped in and rode away, pedaling to the next person and gliding to a stop. I peered back at the old lady. Her shirt faded from red to white. Big red letters appeared on her chest, "BLAME." Wow is all that came to mind. Cool shirt. It was like a mood ring.

Standing before me was a jolly-looking fellow. His big bright, red cheeks looked like they could process a lot of info, like a squirrel with nuts. He gave a warm welcome and asked, "Are you climbing the mountain?"

"I am." I said. "If I climb the mountain, she'll stay with me."

"Who is she?" Rosy cheeks asked.

"My wife. Yeah, my wife asked me for a divorce. One day out of the blue, out of nowhere. I mean straight out of left field. She's hugging me and leans into my ear and asks me to leave. 'Just leave,' she said. 'Like divorce leave.' I asked if she meant like divorce leave, and she said yeah.

Chubby cheeks asked, "What did you do?"

"I went surfing with my son. You know, we have kids. I do things with my kids. I do everything with my kids. Time flies. I don't want to miss a moment." I kept talking. Again, I could not stop talking. "Who quits a marriage? It's a bond. It's a contract between two people. I don't drink. I'm not abusive. I'm so boring I goto bed at 9pm."

Chubby cheeks listened as I jabbered on. I thought, I like this guy. He listened. He's probably a great husband. He didn't interrupt and try to solve my problems. He just listened. "I just don't get it. I was a good husband. Right? You heard my story? Right? How was date night supposed to be fun when you're exhausted from your day? Here we are with a great life, and she wants to end it."

"Want some advice?" he asked.

"I'm listening." I loved this guy's tattoo. He didn't seem like a guy who would have a tattoo. I was wondering what his tattoo meant. Probably some Zen Buddhist symbol.

"If you stop and tell your story to everyone, you'll never make it to the top."

I couldn't understand what he meant, so I asked, "What does your tattoo mean?"

"Acceptance."

"I love the color and simplicity."

I clipped into my pedals and rode away. When I looked back, I saw his red shirt turn white, and bright red letters appeared on it. "DENIAL."

I stood on my pedals with all my might. They were stuck, no

movement. I pushed with every ounce of strength I possessed, but I wasn't going anywhere. My tires were stuck to the road. I had to keep moving, I told myself. I pushed with all my strength and moved inch by inch as my tires made an ooey, gooey sound, and strings of glue stretched from the road to my tire like a spider web.

I looked behind me to the sea of people wearing red shirts that had turned white.

Each shirt displayed a different word in red letters. I couldn't see the faces of the people; all I could see was the bright red letters spelling out, sadness, fear, hate, anger, and forgiveness. As I looked at all the people, I felt so alone. I felt empty. I kept wondering where my friends were. My eyes scanned through all the people, and within them, I spotted Charlie. He stood out from all the rest, like a giraffe with dogs. He went from being far away to right next to me in an instant. I struggled and pushed my pedals to move slowly across the glue within the pavement. Charlie walked beside me with ease. He wasn't walking in glue. I didn't get it. Why wasn't he struggling? Why didn't his feet stick to the asphalt? I was moving slower than a snail.

Charlie gave me a gentle pat on the back. A soothing pulse of energy shot through my body.

"How many people did you tell your story to?" He asked.

I stopped. My legs were fried. I couldn't pedal any farther. The cool thing was, I didn't have to put my feet down. The glue held me in place. I looked back before I answered Charlie's question.

"I told all those people. I told anyone and everyone who would listen. They listened to me. I was amazed at how nice everyone was." Charlie walked to the side of the road. He picked up one of the people and carried them over. Their red shirt had turned to white, in big red letters read, "Sadness."

The person was a cardboard cutout. I told everyone my story, and they were not real. They were merely cardboard cutouts. How could this be? The word sadness began to flash. The light of the word grew in brightness and was quite blinding. The word changed as I squinted my eyes to read it. The sign flashed: fear, failure, anger, denial, sadness, forgiveness... It flashed so brightly that all I could see was spots. The spots floated like balloons across the sky, and in a second, they were the size of hot air balloons with flashing words displayed on their baskets. The letters on the baskets scrolled around as I read: fear, sadness, anger, self-hate, courage, acceptance... Charlie spoke to me, but I couldn't hear him. I didn't know what he was saying. He turned the cardboard cutout away from my eyes and the blinding light faded. The hot air balloons faded into the sky. There was so much noise in my head that I couldn't hear his words until he got louder and louder.

"West! West! West!" The noise in my head became quiet as he asked, "Why are you riding uphill?"

I felt like this was the dumbest question I had ever heard. Why would you ask me such an absurd question? I thought.

He asked again, "Why are you riding up the mountain?"

"To be with my wife," I said. "If I ride to the top, I get her back."

He said, "I'm bewildered by the fact you would ride uphill. You're not in flow."

I interrupted, "The old lady told me, 'Go to the top, and you'll get your wife back. You'll get your family back.' That's why I'm climbing the mountain."

Charlie spoke with a directness. He was calm. I wasn't sure I understood him. He asked, "So you're listening to a cardboard cutout?"

I answered, "Yes!"

"West," Charlie said. "You read the sign, but you didn't read the sign." Once again Charlie didn't make complete sense to me. I gazed down the road filled with white shirts and cardboard cut-outs lining the moonlit road. A solid white stripe split the road in two and wound its way to the bottom. Charlie said, "Your journey is not up the mountain. You'll need all your strength to face your sadness, anger, hate..."

My body was cold. It felt stiff. Tears rumbled off my face. Charlie gently put his hand of comfort on my back.

"Allow yourself to flow as you face the challenges ahead."

I didn't know what to do. "How?"

Charlie spoke with confidence and love. "Take the first step."

I felt wronged. I felt blindsided. I felt paralyzed. The cold of the night consumed my body. Charlie's words echoed in my head. "Take the first step." Two words echoed after.

"What if..?" I asked Charlie, "What if I encounter sadness?"

He answered without hesitation. "I'll be there."

"What if I encounter fear?" I asked.

"I'll be there."

"What if I encounter anger?"

Again he said, "I'll be there."

"What if I kill myself?"

With pure love, he replied, "I'll be there... before you make that commitment."

Charlie spoke in a way that made life feel simple and easy. He made me feel at ease. With a smile, he said, "What if you coast down and discover fear, anger, self-destruction, courage, acceptance, forgiveness, and love?" His body exuded an immense amount of love. "West. What if you found love? What would that feel like? What would that feel like? It's really a simple decision. You can flow down the river, or you can battle your way up."

"Really?" I asked. "You think it's that simple? You think a big, beautiful rainbow is going to show up? And poof, we're riding unicorns and running around naked?"

"I do, West." Charlie didn't waiver. "I do. If that's what you really want?" I tried to grasp what he was saying. "West. I didn't say it would be easy. I said keep it simple."

I was overwhelmed with sadness, consumed by it, numb.

"Charlie. I just want my family back."

"That may not happen."

I raised my voice in fear, anger, and sadness. "Charlie, I just want my family back."

Charlie maintained his loving but firm tone.

"West, That may not happen."

I looked up the mountain to an abyss of darkness and then down the moonlit road. Charlie looked me in the eyes with his piercing blue, soulful eyes. They seemed to glow from behind.

"West, This is your time now. You'll never get it back. Make one simple decision." His voice echoed in my head. Over and over, I heard him say, simple decision, simple decision...

"How do I know I can trust you?" I asked.

"How do you know you can't? I'm your guide."

"Like a tour guide?"

He nodded.

"Well, this is the worst fuckin' tour I've ever been on."

He gazed with a crazy grin.

"West, we're just getting started."

A blaring noise erupted as he finished speaking. Oh my god it was loud and obnoxious. The noise was absurd. I felt like it was an alarm clock I wanted to smash. I can't find it. I reached everywhere and found the noise as I stared at the world's largest clock. I thought I was lying down. Nope. I was standing before a clock that was bigger than I, staring at the face of the clock that had words for numbers. I read in the 12 o'clock position, sadness. The 2 o'clock position read, fear. I saw anger, hate, courage, acceptance, forgiveness, and love.

The sound of the annoying alarm and the words sent shock waves through my body. I launched a big spinning back kick into the snooze button. I felt like Bruce Lee. I knocked the button off the clock and watched it smash to the ground. The clock's hands froze on denial. I watched it slowly fade to sadness. The clock's face became a mirror, covering up all the words. I peered into the mirror and couldn't see myself. I stood there holding a giant black sharpie pen. It was huge. I had to hold it with both hands.

On the mirror, I wrote, "I don't want to be you anymore." I dropped the sharpie to the ground and read my words. I read them again out loud. "I don't want to be you anymore."

I was startled when the clock spoke to me in a clear and deep voice. "I don't want to be you anymore." Its laugh was filled with deep sadness.

"Why are you laughing at me?" I asked the clock.

"The laugh is the sadness that fills your soul," the clock replied. "The laugh is the rejection. The laugh is your denial. The laugh is the mask of West."

I didn't want to hear what this stupid clock had to say. I didn't do anything to deserve this. I stared deep into the mirror and couldn't find myself. I closed my left eye and then closed my right one. I closed both my eyes and opened them quickly. I was nowhere to be found.

The mirror spoke.

"You'll have to go deep to find yourself." I had no clue what he was talking about. In my confusion I turned around to see a table sitting in the middle of the forest. The table was dressed in all white linens, perfectly placed within the trees, which stretched to the sky. They went to infinity without letting the sky show all its essence. I knew the sky was there in a surreal like manner and the sun's rays pierced a small opening through the branches with its glory and sliced a piece of light onto the table. I was in awe as I sat at the table. The silence was broken as the waiter stood in front of me. He was an old man who appeared to have worked past his prime by about a thousand years. His eyes gleamed with a crystal-blue color.

"Hi West," he said, and I was surprised that he knew my name.

When I asked, he said "Lucky guess," and gestured to the vacant seat, "Are you expecting someone?"

I looked down at my watch and then looked up to answer his question. My wife sat before me. I watched as she transformed in front of me. Her hair was longer and changed from black to blond.

I asked, "What happened to your hair?"

Although I could see her lips moving, I was engulfed in silence. The silence was dead quiet with a slight hum from being too quiet. She spoke, and I couldn't hear. I tried to tell her by waving my arms in front of her to get her attention.

"I can't hear you!" I felt so frustrated.

The waiter approached the table and stood by my side. He pointed to two buttons placed in front of me. I didn't notice the two big buttons that were the size of my fist. They appeared weird and out of place. Given the fact that we were in the middle of the forest. Everything felt out of the ordinary.

"Use the buttons to accept what she says, or you can deny it." The waiter pointed with his long finger. "Use the buttons to accept what she says, or you can deny it." He repeated as if I had not heard the first time.

His finger had force behind it. I wanted it and him out of my personal space.

I said, "I got it. I got it. I got it." Then I asked, "Where's the frustration button?" I looked across the table to see if Dawn had buttons. I needed to know if she had buttons, and the only person to ask was the waiter. "Excuse me," I said. "Waiter."

He was right back in my space. Why did he have to stand so close? He raised his eyebrows as he looked down at me.

"Yes. How may I be of service to you?"

I pointed across the table. "Where are her buttons?" What buttons does she get to push?"

The waiter looked at me as if I had asked the dumbest question in the world. "Buttons? She already pushed her buttons. "This is all about you. You. You. You."

"Stop," I said. "Frickin' stop. Do you always repeat yourself?"

The waiter reached down to the table with his extended pointer finger and tapped my hand that was resting on a button labeled, "Repeat."

My own finger looked so fat and bulbous. My hands didn't look like my hands. The moment was soon interrupted as the waiter spoke. "West?"

"Yes" I said. The waiter gestured toward Dawn. "She has been speaking for twenty minutes, and you have listened to nothing." He asked, "Do you want to know what she is saying? If you do, hit the repeat button."

"And if I don't want to know?"

"Hold it down so you can experience the same results, over and over and over."

I was so over listening to him rattle on.

"I have a question, Mr Waiter." I tapped the deny button. "Does this include you?"

He looked at me with his hands on his hips. "My house, my rules."

"Have you looked around?" I asked him. "We're outside."

"Does it really matter?" He paused for a moment. "West. You're stuck in your own little bubble, and you don't realize it. You could be inside or outside. It doesn't matter because you really can't see or feel."

This waiter frustrated me so much that I wanted to leave. I could see that I was outside. What was this dude talking about? I slid back in my chair and stood up. I didn't get far. I hit my head on a clear ceiling and stood there, hunched over. I was trapped. I felt trapped. I felt frustrated.

The waiter asked, "How are you?"

I felt like I was in a game that I didn't want to be a part of. I looked at Dawn as she ate pancakes. This entire scene did not make sense. I answered him curtly, "I'm fine. Just fine."

"Fine?" He asked.

"Yeah, fine."

"Do you know what fine means?"

I wanted this guy to stop talking to me.

"Tell me."

"You are Fucked up, Insecure, Neurotic and Emotional."

I sat in silence for a moment and hoped that this guy vanished from our table. Here came his annoying voice again. "Did you hear me?"

I raised my eyebrows. "Yes. I heard you."

"Did you ever hear your wife tell you she didn't feel loved?" He asked. "Did you ever feel your wife say that?"

I watched my wife eat her pancakes. The moment was so surreal and out of character for her. I heard the waiter. I didn't know what to say.

"Loved? Maybe she didn't feel loved because all she cared about was work. I got no respect from her. Zero. I gave up my career. I took care of our kids. I cooked our meals. I thought I did it with love, or maybe I didn't. I listened to her bitch endlessly about work. And what did I get? A worn-out wife!"

The waiter asked, "What did she get? Did she receive unconditional love?"

I answered, "How could I love her? When she didn't love herself." The waiter asked with a voice that penetrated my soul, "So you cut her off? You became the ice cream man? One big arctic freeze. So, guess what? You put your marriage in the freezer. Your wife took away her respect for you, and you froze your love."

I looked at him and realized he might be right. Unfortunately, it didn't take away the pain, nor did it get my family back. The waiter's words went on repeat in my head: no love, no respect, no respect, no love...

2
FEAR

"Fear is an inner belief you can feed or embrace"

I was standing in front of the restaurant holding my valet ticket. I watched couples exit the restaurant while holding hands, kissing, laughing, and loving life.

Me. I want to go home. I'm just not sure where home is.

They say, home is in the heart. One problem.

My heart is shattered. My heart has imploded.

I guess "THEY" were wrong.

Home is a war zone in my mind that has been obliterated.

In the distance, I hear the familiar sound of a motorcycle racing down the street. Charlie's motorcycle. And in an instant I was wearing my helmet and goggles. It was magic, and I didn't question it. I felt a small amount of comfort wearing the old leather helmet that smelled of rotten guts. I really didn't care. I was truly fascinated by the goggles. They were cool, they made me feel cool, and at the moment, I'd wear anything that made me look and feel cool. I felt like a WWI fighter pilot.

The army green, old-school motorcycle screeches to a halt

with its sidecar attached. Charlie lifts his aviator goggles and shoots me a grin. I take a moment to stare at the sidecar. It looks really old and rickety.

Charlie barks, "Are you climbing aboard?" I look at the condition of the bike and sidecar. They've definitely seen some miles, maybe a few too many. I'm really apprehensive about getting into the sidecar. I think, what a piece of shit. Charlie looks at me wide eyed. I think he heard my thought.'

"This bike has been around the world," he barks. "This bike is the world."

"Yeah," I say, "It's quite evident. Perhaps more than a few times."

"West." Charlie cocks his head to the side. This bike carries stories. It houses fears, love, and laughter. It has character. The seat cradles my ass perfectly. The dents in the gas tank hold my knees. The hum of the engine will soothe you like being in the womb.

I point to my helmet. "And this thing? That smells like pig guts."

Charlie snickers. "I got that at a yard sale. It just looks cool." He waves his arm over the sidecar like a magic wand. "Let's go. It's time for the show. West, climb aboard."

And just like that, I am sitting in the sidecar. I reach for the handle on the dash and grip it firmly with both hands. I read a quote that is etched into the metal above the bar. "Fear Not - God Has A Plan." I read this and can't help but wonder what the fuck it means. I'm wondering who the fuck God really is. For all I know, it's this crazy ass who's driving me. Plan? What plan? I went to Catholic school where Sister Mary told me God's plan was to send me to hell for peeping up her dress. My friends and I wanted to see if it was true that Nun's don't have vaginas.

Maybe this is it. Maybe Charlie is driving me to hell. He guns the engine and off we go, the wind rushing across my face as we ride through the night. The lights around me turn to tracers. The motion is out of control for me. The sensation of wind and my inability to focus on objects allow fear and panic to creep into my existence. I feel out of control. I feel I have no control. I squeeze the "Oh Shit" bar with both hands and read the words etched into the dash. "Fear Not - God Has A Plan."

I'm thinking the person who really needs the plan is the maniac riding the motorcycle. I yell, "Charlie! What's the plan?" He pulls his hands from the handle bars and lies back on the seat. He looks like he could take a nap. I'm screaming inside. My words won't come out. "What the hell are you doing?"

Charlie says with utter calmness, "Here's what we're going to do. I spoke to Jesus."

"Jesus?" I interrupt him.

"West. He was the waiter."

I'm dumbfounded.

"Are you talking about the waiter who locked me in a box?"

"Yes. And technically, you locked yourself in that box. West, today is a big day for you. I'm taking you to fear."

I point to the sign on the dash. "How can I be in fear, if God already has a plan?"

Charlie sits back on the motorcycle as we travel at incredible speeds. The wind stops. The air around us is still. I can hear everything so clearly.

"West," he says. "The plan tonight is you're giving a talk to

1,000 people about love, spirituality, and relationships."

"No," I scream, and add, "Fuck no!"

Charlie doesn't say a word, doesn't dispute my outbursts. He's in the zone. I'm in a tailspin.

"Charlie. I'm not doing it! Sister Mary said God's plan for me was hell. Just take me straight to hell."

Charlie speaks with utter calmness, "There's no such place as hell, and congratulations, West. You're seminar is sold out!"

I'm truly freaking out. The thought of public speaking is debilitating. I'm having an out-of-body experience. There's nothing I can do to help myself. I don't want to give a seminar. I couldn't give a speech to preschoolers. Why would Charlie do this to me? I can't allow some guy to show up in my life and take over. This is crazy. He's obviously crazy. I'm jumping off the motorcycle. It's easy. I've watched stunt guys jump and roll. That's all I need to do, jump and roll. Charlie lies there watching me struggle with my inner thoughts. I think he can read my mind. I can't even imagine standing up to a crowd of people and sharing whatever the hell I'm supposed to share. I've got nothing to share. Who gives a shit about what I have to say. I want off the frickin' crazy train. I stand up in the sidecar with my rear foot in the seat and my front foot braced on the dash. I lean into the wind and turn to Charlie.

"Go faster! Speed up!" Did I just say what I think I said? Have I completely lost my mind. I watch Charlie slip into crouched position and feel the thrust of the bike. Charlie is crouched so low that his head is resting on the gas tank.

He turns to the side and yells to me, "I got her pegged, West! Don't worry! We're gonna make it. Charlie's never late. I'm a high-performance driving machine."

Charlie couldn't have timed it better. The engine back fires, sputters, and quits. The high-performance driver blew the motor. We're coasting, and I'm celebrating. I hold my hands high in the air. I look like Rocky with my fists held high. Bam! The roar of the motor engulfs the silence, and the torque of the engine tosses my ass into the seat. My excitement turns to agony in a flash. A feeling of desperation and helplessness overtake my body. Charlie looks at me with pure joy as the wind blows through his hair and across his face.

"West, this bike has a huge reserve. We can go forever." He points to the small glove box, and says, "Open it." I reach to the dash and push the button with my thumb. I can see a white stack of papers in the box. Charlie makes a gesture with his hand for me to pull them out, "I wrote your speech for you. It's the least I can do since I sprung this event on you so soon."

I grab the papers with my fist and pull them out of the box. I lift my hand into the wind and let the papers fly.

"Oh Shit, Charlie, they just blew away!"

The papers float in slow motion and suspend themselves over us. I can read the words as I watch them float above me. The letters of the words are big and bold in black ink. I read: I am love. I am forgiveness. I am whole. I am acceptance.

They might as well be written in Spanish. I don't get it, and I don't want it. Charlie points to the box again.

"West, don't worry. I made extra copies."

Great I think. Doesn't this guy know I'm okay with failure? I try to close the glovebox, but it won't let me. The papers fly out one by one in slow motion. Each card suspends in front of me as if it's making me read it. The first card says, "I am happy." The second card does the same thing. I read it, "I am happy." Another card comes out, "I am happy." The cards come out one and pause long enough for me to read each one. "I am happy."

Darkness has engulfed us and I feel as though we're moving. We're not. We're parked on a stage. I look to my right at a huge projection screen. I look to my left at a black velvet curtain. Lights from above gently fade up, and I'm in the spotlight. The massive video screen projects a video count down starting from 5 4 3 2 1.

I'm watching myself on screen with my newborn son and wife. We look young and happy as we play with the baby in bed. The room is bright with golden pillows and white sheets. Dawn and I look so happy with the baby, a big chunky boy. A tear rolls down my cheek as I watch this beautiful memory. Life seemed so simple then. Life was simple. It wasn't easy having a baby, but it was simple. I'm crying. I feel the tears run down my face as I gaze upon the screen. This is a moment in time that will never be seen. I lie in bed while on my back with my legs stretched to the sky. I hold my son high in the air, perched upon my feet with delicate care. He grows before my eyes, becoming a three-year-old in an instant. Dawn appears through the course of this growth. Each time she appears, her hair has changed, her clothes have changed. My clothes stay the same during this short evolution of time. I watch as I see her smile go away as did mine too. We each went from smiling with the baby to walking through the motions. The moments move fast and are surreal. Dawn stands before me as her belly grows in size. We hug but we don't embrace. I can hear my thoughts as I watch the screen. They're not directed at anyone. They're spoken in a monotone. I know I'm happy to have another baby. I'm ready to welcome the child with unconditional love. I wasn't ready for the emotional wear and tear it took to conceive the child. Dawn had drained me of all my existence. The energy and planning it took far exceeded my capacity as a human, and my wife had made it a job. She pushed hard during times of ovulation. Her intensity depleted my drive. I longed for another child. I wanted to have more kids. I wanted to do it with grace and spontaneity. The passion was gone. I was punching the clock and looking for my lunch break. I wanted her to get pregnant so the job would end. The job should have been exciting and fun. It should have been my dream job.

I stare at the screen, looking at her beautiful belly and think about the amazing child that came from that belly. She's a child filled with passion and drive. Maybe I wasn't punching the clock. Maybe that's how I felt and didn't talk about it. I kept it pent up. I didn't know how to express what was taking place. I was stuck. Emotions rush over me as I reflect upon this time period.

The screen shows me standing on the corner of a busy city street. I'm holding a huge phone with a massive screen that everyone can read. People walk past quickly all the while staring at me. I see them, and we lock gazes as they pass by The screen on the phone reads, "Get home now! I'm ovu--lating! My brain is screaming, "GO! GO! GO!" The crowd is screaming, "GO! GO! GO!" My legs won't move. I try with all my strength to move my legs. No way. They're not moving. I'm stuck. Anxiety races in the pit of my stomach. I want to puke. I need help. My lips are sealed. My soul is closed. I'm not asking for help.

I don't know how to ask. The crowd is roaring, "GO! GO! GO!" The feeling is debilitating. The feeling is overwhelming. The feeling is death. My brain screams run! My legs are stuck. My legs won't move. The anxiety deep within the pit of my stomach is swirling and heavy. The weight holds me back, and the swirl makes me want to puke. I hate the feeling. I need to puke. I thought making babies was supposed to be fun. Where's the fun? My world is spinning. My mind is spinning so fast I need to puke. I put my hands on my knees and close my eyes as I try to purge my emotions. Nothing comes out. Nothing I pull in a deep breath as I stand up. I'm in my living room, and there before me is Dawn. She stands there in her lacy lingerie, talking a million miles per hour. I'm anxious. I'm hot. I'm sweating. It feels as though I'm on the job interview of my life.

I hear her screaming and talking so fast, "Let's go! Let's go! Get your clothes off! I'm ovulating!" I'm desperately trying to fulfill her wish or command, I'm not sure which. My clothes feel stuck to my body. They're not coming off. She's talking so fast, "You took so long to get home. My window is closing."

"Your window is closing, like your vagina is closing up shop?" I ask.

I think what if the window slams down on my dick? I'm so confused. I can't get my clothes off. Dawn's voice is tripping off her tongue a million miles per hour. I really can't understand her. I get it, we're supposed to be making a baby. Where's the love? Where's the fun? She rips off my T-shirt. She rips off my shorts and looks at my manhood.

"Let's go! Get it up! Come on, get it up!"

I stand there defeated as all the emotion gets sucked out of the room. The room is filled with silence as crocodile tears stream down her face. I watch the tears drip from her cheeks. I have nothing to give, not even a hug. I'm numb. I'm emotionless. I pull my shorts back on and try to figure out what just happened. I see the anger in her face. I see the disappointment in her face. She spews the disappointment on me with her hands as she slams me in the chest.

She yells so quietly, "It's all your fault."

All I can think is, "Fuck you! Who needs all this pressure?"

The lights on the stage dim as a spotlight pierces my eyes. I'm blinded by the intensity as I begin to rise while sitting in the sidecar. I'm being raised into the air, and the spotlight intensifies and blinds my vision. All I can see are specks of light floating in the air. I'm blinded. Where is Charlie? The roar of the audience engulfs me.

They chant, "Pressure. Pressure. Pressure. Pressure." The chant mixed with the blinding light while being raised into the sky is making me feel delirious and completely out of control. I'm well above the audience while feeling trapped in the sidecar. The lights are now flashing to the beat of the audience chanting, "Pressure."

A second of silence fills the room. A soft golden glow radiates from the screen as a beautiful baby girl miraculously floats into view. You can fill the love emanating from her innocence. The crowd in unison lets out a groan. The emotion is peaceful. The emotion is love. Both my kids are now on screen. Zang, my son, is holding Emma, his baby sister, with pure joy. The moment is priceless and filled with love. The essence is intoxicating to myself and the audience. I'm in a trancelike state as I gaze at my two beautiful children grown into teenagers. The rate of growth is exponential. It's happening so fast that I can't fathom the change. I feel anxiety race through my body as I gaze at the screen. The moment seems both real and out of my control. I feel stuck. I'm stuck in this stupid sidecar on a stage perched high in the air. How is this possible? I don't want to sit here. I would like for somebody to get me the fuck out of here. Enough. I've had enough.

The screen rolls back to a time of me teaching my son to ride his bike. We've pulled the training wheels off. I've given him a push from behind to get the bike rolling. He holds the handlebars with confidence as his strong chubby legs push the pedals with ease. Pride exudes from his face as his thick blond hair flows out the side of his helmet. The helmet straps push his fat cheeks up to create all the cuteness in the world. Nothing matters in this moment except his bliss for riding the bike. I watch with pride and joy as he pedals down the street with exuberance.

My daughter appears at my side wearing a blue dress with dance shoes on. Music swirls in the air, and we can't help but dance. The music moves our bodies and feet to the beat. She twirls with such grace and poise as if God is directing the perfect little dancer. I hold her hands, as we spin round and round with laughter. Zang rides his bike in circles around us as we dance and laugh. We're aging as I watch the screen. Zang's bike tires have created a perfect worn path in the grass that circles us.

They grow to young teenagers, and everything changes. The bike Zang rides shift many times to become a full size bicycle. In the end, he is riding without a helmet. He's a young man riding his bike in a circle while Emma and I continue to Dance. Emma changes outfits a dozen times and grows into a beautiful young woman with with long reddish-blond hair flowing down her back.

The golden sun shines upon us as the three of us play in it's radiant glow. My daughter's age went from three to twelve in an instant, and my son went from six to fifteen. The green grass is growing faster and faster, at an alarming rate. I've never seen grass grow so fast. I have become the observer as my children continue to dance and play. They continue to move through the tall grass with ease, but in my mind, I think it should be hard. They move effortlessly. It's truly like magic as I watch my daughter dance with elegance and beauty. My son rides in a circle as if nothing is holding him back.

The tranquil moment is broken as Dawn enters the grass. She doesn't look mad or happy. Her face is still, expressionless, and she carries a small box with both hands. The three of them come together in the middle of the grass. The kids gather around her as she lifts the lid on the off-white decorative box wrapped in purple and gold strands. Dawn slowly lifts the lid as bright white light spills from the box.

The light dances in color as it swirls around the children in purple and gold. I want to be a part. I can't. I don't know how to get there. I watch as the kids are consumed by the swirling strands of light. It's as if they are intoxicated. There presence is slipping away from me, and I don't know what to do. The voice in my head is screaming at me. "Go get them!" I don't have the power. My legs are frozen. My voice is stuck in my throat. The only voice screaming and demanding is in my head. "Go get them! She is taking them! You will never see them again!"

They are all three being consumed by the power of the light. The moment should be magical, but not for me. I'm using all my strength to stand up. I'm strapped down. Why are there straps going across my shoulders? I'm really confused as to why I'm being held down. I reach with my right hand to free myself. The strap doesn't move. My frustration level is huge.

"How can this be?" I feel the panic consuming my body as the weight of the straps holds me in place as my lips move but no words come out. Nobody can help me. Nobody can hear me. My voice rages inside my head, "I need help! Somebody help me!"

Why is this happening to me? She can't take my kids! Those are my kids! The purple and gold light grows in size as the kids consume it's energy. I can't see their faces. I can't hear their voices. I can't do anything to save them. I need to save them. Is she putting a spell on them? They dance in the love of the light, and I think yes, they're being consumed by the grips of a spell. I can't see their happiness because I'm stuck in my own misery and self-pity. I feel excruciating heat in my face as I continue with my struggle to free myself and rescue my children. The voice in my head screams, "I'm their dad! I'm their dad!" The purple and gold light consumes them as the grass grows around them. I can no longer see them. They have disappeared into the depths of nowhere. The thought of loss catapults my energy for one last burst of strength and allows me to break loose from the straps. I launch from the grips of nylon and shoot myself into the sky as if I am shot from a cannon.

I'm flying. I have taken flight with the thought of finding my children. The grass below me moves with the swirl of the light.

I can hear my children's laughter.

"Where are they? I can hear them. I can't see them. Are they laughing or crying?"

I have a chance to find them. I have been given a second chance to find them. I have been given the strength to find them. I'm hovering over the tall green grass as I search desperately to see them. I spot a bright red door in the grass that separates me from my children. I have to fly through the door and push myself to the other side. I have one option, and this is it. I aim for the door with all my focus. The wind is rushing past my face and body. I start to question my ability to get through the door.

"Am I going to make it? What if I don't make it?"

The voice in my head takes over. "You're a failure!" The voice is louder. "You're shit! You're nothing! You're an embarrassment! Who the fuck do you think you are?"

I slam into the door with the force of a mouse. I don't think I even made a noise as I hit it. It didn't budge.

The voice is louder. "See you're weak! You're shit! You're embarrassing!"

I sit there surrounded by the grass and staring at the ground. I was flying. I was superman for a brief second. And now I'm nothing. I'm a lifeless, broken human being who can't find himself. The loss of my children is debilitating and overwhelming for my spirit.

On the other side of the door stands a man I haven't seen in a long time. He's big, strong, and scary. It's my father holding the door closed. He speaks with judgement that rips my soul apart and leaves it shattered in pieces.

"West. You're a fucking failure. You should have blown right through that door. What a little pussy you are. What a piece of shit. I'm ashamed to know you. I'm more ashamed now than the time you missed the game winning free-throw in sixth grade. What a little loser!"

His voice echoes through the cells of my body. I can't escape his grip. He is strong and powerful, and he's right. I am nothing.

"How do you miss such an easy shot?" he continues. "You know, when I humiliated you in front of the entire gym, I thought that would motivate you to not be in the situation you're in now. The humiliation you felt while shooting free-throws in the gym while I screamed at you should drive you to be a better person. It should drive you to be a man. My God you're a failure!" He won't stop talking, his voice loud and bold. My body wilts as he verbally beats me once again. "No wonder your wife is leaving. You bounced off that door like an under-cooked noodle."

I sit on the ground, listening to this asshole totally degrade me. I have nothing to say. Everything he said was true. I am lifeless. I am thoughtless. The three most valuable pieces of my life are gone. My fear of loss has come true.

The familiar roar of Charlie's motorcycle comes to a screeching halt. He slides to a stop right in front of the door. He lifts his goggles to his forehead and stares at me with confidence. His presence alone puts me at ease with his slight glow of golden light that surrounds him. He seems Jesus like, and I'm not a religious person. He slides off the motorcycle with such ease, he looks majestic as he walks to the door. Then he twists the door knob.

"Why do you do things the hard way?" he asks, as he opens the door. "I find it so bizarre that you would try to fly through the door instead of twisting the knob and walking through it."

His eyes pierce my soul and scan every cell in my body. It doesn't feel invasive. More like he needs to give me answers. I don't have questions though. I don't know what to ask. He offers me his thoughts, but they aren't really thoughts. He just knows.

"West, you're housing so many limiting beliefs about yourself that need clearing. I could hear your thoughts from a mile away." I sit there feeling defeated and exhausted. One big tear rolls down my cheek. It feels like a beachball rolling down my face. I think to myself, I'm scared. I'm flat out scared and I don't know what to do.

Charlie says, "Are you asking me for help?"

I look up from the ground. "Yes. I'm asking for your help. I need help. I'm so in fear of life that I feel helpless. Can you help me?"

Charlie releases the biggest sigh I've ever heard. "I can't help you, your inner beliefs are tattooed to your soul. I heard you say you're worthless. I heard you say you're a piece of shit. I heard you say you're ashamed. I heard you say you're a failure. I heard you say you have no value. Those are just a few thoughts I've heard you spit out about yourself. West, you're eroding your soul. You put those tattoos on your soul. They're a lifetime of stories that you created, and since you created them, they must be true. Are they?"

"I don't know," I answer.

Charlie looks at me with powerful presence. "West, true or not true, all that matter is that you set your intent to create a great story, a story that will make your Grandchildren be in awe of you. Create a story surrounded in love, West. Love is the most powerful emotion you can operate from." Charlie holds his hand down by the ground.

He pats the ground. "West, you're operating at a low. You're living in fear. You've allowed your treasure chest of beliefs to feed your fear. It's time to open the chest. It's time to live in love. It's time to create an amazing life."

I take a big breath in and release it. I understand what Charlie is saying and really try to open the chest that he referenced.

Charlie gestures to the door. "Up first. You're going to thank your dad for everything." The thought of facing my dad makes me uncomfortable, but Charlie calls for him anyway.

"Pops, please come forward."

Pops walks through the door wearing short jean shorts and a T-shirt from the seventies. He doesn't look as scary as I remember, and his outfit is kinda funny. He stands there with his hands on his hips and his big Burt Reynolds mustache.

Charlie looks at me. "Go ahead, West, ask him why he humiliated you?"

I'm timid, but I ask, "Why did you make me shoot those free throws in front of the entire gym? Why did you punch me in the head? I missed. I know I missed. I felt like a loser for missing. Why were you harsh?"

Pops stands there with calmness as if he has knowledge I never knew or he has changed. He speaks clearly.

"I failed in sports. I didn't want you to fail. My dad wasn't there for me. He never came to games. I did it to make you stronger. I did what I thought was right. I'm sorry."

And just like that, Pops fades away. I want to desperately accept his apology and move on, but unfortunately it wasn't enough. I feel unsettled by his simple explanation with an apology.

That's it. That's all I get?

Charlie asks, "Did you just ask if that's all you get?"

"Charlie, are you listening to my thoughts?" I demand.

"West," he says. "Your thoughts are really loud. What more do you want from the guy? He gave you everything he could."

"He gave me nothing," I say. "He's a soulless human who gave his family nothing but an ass kicking. He's an animal who beat my mom and kicked my ass every chance he could. So what do I want from him? I want to know why? Why did he kick my mom's ass? What kind of man beats a woman? What kind of man beats his kid? How could he carry so much anger through life? He destroyed our family with his abuse. He destroyed everything. So Charlie, you're telling me I should accept a sorry? Fuck that and fuck him. I don't give a fuck if I ever see that motherfucker again."

I'm mad, angry, defeated. Charlie doesn't fight back. His look gives me the sense everything is going to be all right. The issue I have is, I don't know how it would be all right.

Charlie says, "West, you're going to have to face your past. You're going to have to face the fears, anger, humiliation, failure and shame from your past. Your childhood harbors a lot of emotions that are hidden deep within you."

I sigh and want to believe him, want to believe anything.

"West, you've carried these emotion for way too long," he says. "It's time to take the necessary steps to release your emotional baggage. Your heart and soul needs a tattoo of love. The beauty is that you're capable of retelling your story."

"Charlie, the only story I want to tell is the one of getting my family back."

"You have nothing until you reclaim your soul," he says. "Because until you recapture your life and create a soul filled with love, you will live a life of loneliness, with or without your family. You're stuck in fear. You're stuck in failure. You're stuck in unworthiness."

"What do I do?" I ask him, and he is quiet for a moment.

Finally, he says, "Allow yourself to move out of fear and pick the two things you would like to do that scare the hell out of you. Think about your wildest dream, and let's make it happen."

I draw a big deep breath and say the first two things that come to my mind. "Charlie, my wildest dream would be to surf the biggest wave at Peahi' and get spit out of a barrel that feels like I'm coming out of a cave."

Charlie looks at me with his head nodding yes. "That dream is passion. What else?"

I don't even have to think about it. "Charlie, I want to wing suit fly. I want to soar over the Swiss alps with a group and race through rock formations and have smoke streaming from my ankles."

I can tell he's into my dreams. He's nodding, and getting the visual in his head too.

"West, let's make it happen. Let's do it."

"Can you make it happen without me dying?" I ask.

He pauses, and I feel his energy shift. He scratches his head. "If you don't live your dreams, you're dying." He says.

The fear is present. How could it not be?

"Maybe I should pick two dreams that I can actually do." I tell him, and he smiles.

"Those wouldn't be dreams then. You would become the walking dead. Be your dream. Live your dream. Live the life you want."

Everything he's saying makes sense, but I was still afraid of death, I'm not ready to die. Charlie seems oblivious though.

"It's time to live an extraordinary life," he says. "It's time."

I was ready to feel what Charlie was saying but I couldn't.

He says extraordinary but all I can feel is ordinary.

"Be different," he continues. "Be bold."

All I can hear is the voice of James Earl Jones repeating ordinary. James repeats my limiting beliefs, SHAME, FAILURE, SHITTY HUSBAND, BAD DAD, YOU DON'T DESERVE IT, YOU'RE NOT GOOD ENOUGH and FEAR. The words play in my head, so loud and bold that they feel real. I've been hearing them my whole life, and they're normal. They're mine.

"Have you heard enough?"

I look up to see Charlie with all his wisdom and strength. "West, put your attention on what you want. Put your attention on your dreams."

James's voice made my thoughts feel so real and alive.

"Do you want to go flying first or surfing?" Charlie asks.

"I'm not doing either one. I'm fine."

"I'm sorry," he says. "You've already placed your order. It's time. It's time to trust."

I shake my head and say. "I didn't place an order, and this isn't Amazon. I'm almost certain I said I might want to fly, or I might want to surf. I chose the wing suit merely based on my attraction to Roberta Mancina. When she flies, you can see so much passion exuding from her that it's intoxicating."

"I can see how you would be attracted to her confidence," he says. "I'm here to help you make your dreams come true. You deserve that."

I'm not sure I want to feel deserving. Actually, I don't know what to feel. Everything Charlie is saying to me makes sense while he's speaking, but then when I think about it, I really don't understand anything.

"Do you know the nursery rhyme, Row Row Row Your Boat?" He asks.

"What does that have to do with anything?"

He ignores my sarcasm. "So, what's easier, West? Rowing your boat upstream or downstream?"

"Downstream. A second grader knows that."

"What do you want to do?" He asks. "It's your choice. Easy? Hard? Smooth? Bumpy? It's quite simple."

I'm not sure where he's getting simple from. Nothing about life feels simple. Yeah, I can sing the nursery rhyme, and life feels so simple rowing your boat downstream. Really? That's all I need to do?

"I don't think so." I tell him. "Life is fuckin' hard!"

"It doesn't have to be," he tells me. "Make one decision. Use one word to create a difference. Say yes to fulfilling your dreams. Say yes to facing your fears. Say yes to being a better dad."

"I just want to be a better husband."

"No," he says. "You don't get a do-over. Dawn doesn't want a do-over. It takes two people to want it, to make it, and love it." I sit there confused by what he's saying. I don't know what to do. Charlie's voice is so loud and full of energy. "West, are we going?"

I let out the longest exhale of my life. "Okay. Let's do it"Yes!

Charlie lets out a big hoot, pulls his goggles over his eyes, and pins the throttle wide open. The force of the engine sits me back in my seat as the wind blows in my face. I feel exhilarated that I said yes. It felt damn good. The wind is now so fierce that I'm struggling to see.

"Damn, Charlie! How fast are we going?"

The ride becomes smooth as if we are flying. Did we reach a speed of lift off? We have to be flying. The force of the wind flips off my goggles, and I can't see. Tears stream across my face as I struggle to see with the wind blasting in my eyeballs. All I can think is that Charlie is a madman. A true lunatic. His motorcycle is powered from adrenaline, and the turbos are at one hundred percent. At the moment I think I can't take it anymore, the wind begins to subside. Water droplets hit my face. I lick the side of my mouth and can taste salt. It is all I can do to open my eyes. They feel glued shut from holding all the tension of going so fast. Everything goes silent, and then it's broken by the sound of Charlie's voice.

"See West, dreams do come true."

I peer through the slits of my wind-burned eyelids as my jaw falls open. A giant mountain of water marches toward us. I look left. I look right. "Charlie, you rode your motorcycle into the ocean?"

He stands up on his seat and holds one arm out to sea as if he is presenting me with a gift. "My boy, your dream is now! Allow your desires to unfold and cast your fears to the wind. This is it. Opportunity is staring you in the eyes. Look at that wave. She's a rolling piece of art. Immerse yourself and become one. Come on, man! You said your dream was to get pitted on the biggest wave. Suit up!"

"A little heads up would have been nice," I say.

"Why?" He asks. "So, you could overthink it?"

I'm staring at this mass of a mountain coming at us, and I'm literally shaking with fear. Fear of dying. Fear of failure. Fear of humiliation. Fear of fear. I look at Charlie with terror racing through my veins.

"I don't have a choice, do I?"

"No."

How did this crazy fuck become part of my life?

"You got this," he says. "I'll tow you in with the bike. I got you. Trust me, man. It's all about trust."

I look at the back of the motorcycle and see a yellow tow line stretched behind the bike and a rescue sled attached to the back of the motorcycle. The look of the motorcycle with the rescue sled and tow line sitting in the middle of the ocean is pretty bizarre. Ultimately though, the sound of this mountainous wave crashing captures my attention. As the wave rolls under us, we rise to the clouds and then fall to the backside. My heart is pumping and my entire chest feels like it's beating to a drumming circle. My god, we rise into the clouds and then fall off the backside. My breathing is heavy, my heart pounding, and there sits Charlie, calm and cool.

"West, no matter what, you will succeed."

My thoughts and anxiety are racing.

"Really Charlie? No shit. I will either succeed at the worst wipeout of my life or..."

"It's just a wave."

"Are you kidding me? It's Mount fucking Everest! Look at that thing roll through here. What if I fail? Failure is death!"

"Failure is opportunity to learn, and when we open our hearts to failure and accept our faults, failures, and negative beliefs, we grow," he says. "It's time to face your fears. I'm here for you."

"Really? Easy to say while you sit on your motorcycle."

"What if you could accomplish anything you thought?" He asks. "Would you do it?"

I take a deep breath and hold it as I think about Charlie's question. What if I could accomplish anything? Would I do it?

"I'm going to count backwards from 5," he tells me.

"What? Five?"

Charlie shoves me in the water, and I hear him say "Four" right before my splash. I can't gather my thoughts, but I have the rope in my hand and the board attached to my feet. I look up to Charlie on the bike. He holds up three fingers and then two and then one. I hear the roar of the motorcycle pull me to my feet. I'm up and gliding across the water, effortlessly. My hands loosely hold the handle, and my feet feel at one with the board. All the sounds of the ocean and motorcycle are muted as I'm being towed out to sea. My trust is in Charlie. I can hear his voice.

"Let go and trust God. Let go and trust yourself. Let go and trust me."

Is it really trust? Do I let go of control, or do I move into the I-don't-give-a-fuck-anymore attitude? At this moment, I'm committed to this dream. The voice in my head is screaming, "Stop! Let go! You're too scared! You're a failure! You're a piece of shit! You can't accomplish anything! You're a loser! You're scared of everything. Your fears will run your life!"

"Shut up!" I scream. "Shut the fuck up!" The water is moving faster under my feet. My grip is tighter as the voice in my head gets louder.

"I knew you wouldn't let go."

"Shut up." My voice gets louder.

"I'm always right, whatever I say, you believe."

The wind is moving across my face as water splashes me. I feel out of control. I can't tell if it's daylight or night. The handle feels like a piece of me. Can I even let go of it?

The voice in my head whispers, "Don't let go. I'll keep you safe."

At this moment, I realize I don't want safe. I want to ride the biggest wave of my life. I want to feel the rush of adrenaline as I race down the face of a moving mountain of water and pull into a cavernous barrel and come racing out, as if being shot out of a cannon. That's an adrenaline rush that can last a lifetime. Red smoke engulfs my vision. I know I'm moving. Why does the smoke feel so still? The air feels calm, and so quiet. My head feels heavier with this helmet on. The red smoke has completely impaired my vision. The sounds around me are non-existent. Why am I holding this handle? It feels weird. I want to drop it. I want to throw it. The handle feels like a piece of my body, as if I were born with it. The red smoke is giving me a comforting effect. I feel as though I'm being wrapped in a blanket and being held like a baby. I want to stay in this position.

The silence is broken, and I feel a swoosh of wind pass by my right side and then my left. The swoosh of wind is forceful and also peaceful. I want to follow the peaceful feeling. The red smoke dissipates as two more people race past me and leap from the mountain while wearing wing suits. Golden light cascades across the sky, creating a gentle glow that caresses my soul.

Charlie gently reaches for the handle and whispers, "Let go."

My hands don't hesitate. I release the handle as Charlie and I leap from the mountain top. I spread my arms to the side and allow my suit to catch wind. I am soaring.

Charlie and I fly, side by side, high above the mountains. The wind races across our faces, and Charlie says, "You did it. You left all your fear on the mountain. I'm proud of you."

The feeling is freedom. The feeling is golden. I am soaring, and nothing can stop me. I look out in front of me and can see trails of red, gold, green, and purple smoke streaming from other people who are soaring over the mountains too. I shout, "I did it!"

3
ANGER

"Anger plows the path to self-destruction"

I look at Charlie as we soar over the mountains, and the calmness that resonates from his weathered face. He looks stoic, like nothing can rock his world. I feel as if my face is going to peel off, and my body and my thoughts are completely out of control. How does he do it? The guy is truly amazing. I'm having this weird thought. When I grow up, I want to be like Charlie. The odd part is, I am a grown up. I have a house, car, kids, dogs, fish and a goddamn cellphone that won't stop going off. I stare at Charlie. He has nothing, but really he has it all. Does he have a wife? Does he have a dog? Surely this guy has kids. I bet he has a Golden Retriever. Look how chill he is. He's definitely got a Golden. What the fuck? There goes my phone again. Can I take a call in a wing suit? Can I text? I'm thinking that texting and flying are probably a bad idea, but my phone is driving me crazy. Vibrate. Vibrate. Vibrate. I want to fly! I don't want to hear a phone vibrate. Why do I have this stupid thing. I don't remember binging it. Seriously, I don't want this thing. I'm flying! The freedom feels insane. I gaze at Charlie in awe, he glides through the air as if he's not moving.

He motions for me to follow him, but I disregard him and pull out my phone. The weird part is, I'm not holding my phone. It's attached to my wrist. I'm truly baffled while I stare at my wrist with this appendage. How is thing attached to me? I'm fixated on this stupid piece of electronics. I peer at the screen and see my wife on the screen, flailing her arms with toxic, negative emotion spewing from the phone. I have no idea why she's so angry, and I don't give a fuck. I really don't care. I'm flying with the wind blowing in my face. I have a sense of freedom, and it feels good. I twist my wrist so I don't have to see my phone. Wow, I think. How easy was that? All I had to do was roll my wrist so I didn't have too see this stupid phone. I can get back to flying.

I'm flying. I have set myself free at last, but the feeling is short lived. The peace and freedom is quickly interrupted as my phone spins back in place and is blaring in my face. It's larger this time. It's frickin' huge. My God, the screen is so big I can't hold it up. The monitor is so large and heavy it's going to make me crash. I can't fly with this stupid ass thing hanging on my wrist. Oh god, there's her face again. Dawn's. Jeez. Her face fills the entire screen. I can see her facial muscles flexing in her temples. She looks like a mad lizard who's going to pounce on me.

"Can you stop calling me? I'm flying!"

"You answered the phone!" She says. "You didn't have to answer the phone. Why did you do that if you didn't want to talk?"

"By the way, I didn't answer the phone. You appeared out of no where, thin air. I don't have a clue how you got here. So please leave."

"Why don't you hang up on me?" She asks.

"Because I'm flying! Can you hear me? I'm flying! I'm here with Charlie, enjoying an amazing soar through the atmosphere, and you ring my phone like thirty frickin' times."

"You never answer your phone unless I call a couple of times," she says. "It's not like you're busy. From what I can see, you're doing nothing."

"Can't you see I'm flying?"

"Flying?" She squints at me. "With those ridiculous glasses on? Give me a break. Who wears goggles and a helmet on an airplane? I guess you. What a freak!"

"Airplane?" I shriek. "I'm flying in a wing suit. Remember? I told you, I was going to start flying, but of course you never fuckin' listen."

She hesitates for one second and then asks, "Did you call my mom and sing happy birthday?"

"Yeah, right, when I was flying through the ass crack of the mountain, I thought of your mom. Hell no. I didn't call her. Can you hang up, please? I'd like to fly in peace."

Seriously, I'd really like to do that. I'm staring at the screen, watching her lips move. She keeps talking, but I have no idea what she is saying. My body is so tense and filled with frustration that I could explode or maybe implode.

"Did you feed the dogs?" She asks.

"What dogs? We never had a dog."

"If we had dogs, would you feed them? Because it seems to me, you're just thinking about yourself. Who flies around by themselves? How would the dogs feel if you didn't feed them?"

My frustration level is sky-rocketing.

"You're talking about dogs we don't have, okay? We don't have dogs."

"West, it's Sunday. Did you take out the trash?"

This woman has gone absolutely mad.

"It's not Sunday." I say.

"Then what day is it, West? Did you unclog the toilet in the game room? The kids clogged the toilet again."

"Yeah. I did it ten minutes ago. Didn't you see me? I used your towel to wipe up the dirty toilet water."

"West, what about the dogs? Seriously, are you going to feed them? I also think it would be really cool if you taught the dogs to sing happy birthday to my mom. Could you do that West? She would feel really special if you could do that."

"Yeah. Yeah I can do that. As soon as I make dinner. I'll teach our imaginary dogs to fart happy birthday."

Holy crap, I'm lost in a cloud. I can't see. All I hear is the wind rushing through my ears, and my cheeks flutter with the speed of the air racing past my skin. This huge screen on my wrist is weighing me down. It's making my flight not fun. The freedom of flying has dissipated. Where did Charlie go? I'm not looking at that stupid monitor again. I can't look. How stupid is that thing? The thing feels like an anchor attached to my arm. Jeez, it feels welded to my wrist. In the distance, I see a solution for removing the appendage. Yes. Look at the huge rock sticking out. I can fly right below it and let the rock shave this apparatus from my body. The rock can smash this thing. I want to see it fall to the ground in a million pieces. My focus and attention are laser pointed at removing this monitor from my wrist. And although my focus feels good, I fail to read the letters etched into the rock above. I'm flying into another dimension without knowing. The letters read, ANGER. I fly right below the rock and use all my strength to lift the appendage into the rock. Smash, boom, bang! Yes! The monitor explodes into a million pieces and falls to the ground. I am free. Or so I think.

The gateway goes black. I have entered total darkness. The flying has ceased, and I'm walking. Not only is it dark, but it's dead quiet. I hear the crunch beneath my feet as I take steps leading to god knows where. Why did I answer that stupid phone? I was enjoying my moment soaring through the clouds in total peace and harmony. How did this happen so quickly? Why? Did she really ask me to teach our dogs to sing happy birthday? Dogs we don't have? This is ludicrous. I'm in a cave of darkness. I want out. I want out now. My insides are boiling as I'm trapped within this unknowing of nothingness. I can't take it and let out a primal scream. The echo bounces off every square inch of wall and goes forever.

With every step I take, my shoes grow in weight and feel excruciating uncomfortable. How did I end up in this hole of blackness? That frickin' bitch distracted me. She sabotaged me with her incessant texts and calls. What the hell? You couldn't send one? You had to send endless numbers of them? Oh, and stupid me. I should have ignored them all. But no! I didn't. I go from soaring like an eagle to the abyss of nothingness.

Seriously, my feet feel as though I'm standing in concrete crocs. They truly must weigh fifty pounds each. I'm part Dutch. Why wouldn't they be wood? This is hell. I've landed in hell. What am I supposed to do? I can't see my hand in front of my face. This might be the one time I wish that I smoked. At least then I would have a lighter. I need a torch to guide my dumbass out of here. I lose myself in my scream.

"Fuck! Fuck! Fuck! Fuck you, bitch! Once again you fucked me over. Life was good, and you fucked it up!" My scream is so guttural that my voice cracks, and my eyes fill with the pain of life.

I swipe the tears from my eyes and glimpse the faintest shimmer of light deep within the cave. The light gives me hope. The light gives me strength. I can do it. I'm walking. I want to run, but these damn concrete crocs are horrendously heavy. At this pace, I'll be an old man by the time I reach the light. My determination can't drown out the horrendous noise my shoes are making as they drag across the cave floor. It's like dog nails on a chalk board but magnified a thousand times.

The voice in my head is angry. It's screaming at me to go barefoot. Like I really want to wear these stupid ass shoes. I use all my might to bend over and remove the concrete from my feet. Nothing! My body won't allow me to bend over. My entire body is stiff, and feels frozen like the crocs on my feet. I'm like a big walking erection without fun or excitement. Here I am trying to drag myself through a tunnel of darkness to nowhere; thinking only this: How did I get here? It's beyond weird. I'm stuck. My brain is stuck. I know there's an answer but I don't know where to look. I don't know whom to ask. The bizarre part is I think I've been here before. The voice in my head has consumed all the stillness of the cave.

"You're a fucking idiot. Why did you let yourself get to this point? What a fuck head. Jesus Christ, you deserve to be in this mess. Do something with yourself."

It's loud and obnoxious like the screaming at a Super Bowl party. The battle is raging in my head, and I can't find the switch. Where's the music? It could help me drown myself out. Where's Facebook? It will help me get lost. A big bottle of tequila would do the trick. I could gulp that shit down to kill the voices in my head. All I want is quiet. All I want is peace. Why is there concrete on my feet? I don't get it. Is this what Herman Munster felt like trying to walk around? Somebody frickin' help me. God, am I so stupid that I put concrete shoes on? Apparently so. I'm so worked up, I need a drink of water. My anger and rage boil as I scream out.

"Get me the fuck out of here."

I'm panting, out of control as the rage overtakes my being.

My inner voice asks, "Do you remember that song, There's rage in the cage?"

"Yes." I shout. "How's that supposed to help me?"

The voice is annoying me with the questions.

"Are you mad, bro? Why are you mad, bro?"

I'm being taunted and bullied by my own thoughts. Fuck yeah, I'm mad, bro! And I'm not just mad; I'm going mad. My thoughts are consuming me like a tiger on a rat. I'm easy prey. I'm consuming myself.

A faint voice deep within my soul whispers. "You're gonna be ok."

"What? Say that again. I couldn't really hear you."

The moment of silence is abruptly interrupted by the obnoxious voice. "You deserve to be miserable. You deserve all of this. You deserve to be a miserable human being. You deserve to be a miserable, angry man. You deserve to be where you are."

I can't help but wonder, if I deserve to be where I am but don't know where I am, how does that make sense? How long am I supposed to walk with the weight of the world on my feet?

The faint voice within me quietly bellows out, "You're a fighter. You're a warrior. Stop focusing on the weight of the shoes and focus on walking to the light. You have a choice. You can choose where to put your thoughts and energy. Where do you want to put your focus?"

The faint little voice is right. I might be walking slowly, but I'm moving forward. I can do it. I'm going to do it. I stare at the faint light far off in the distance. My eyes are fixated on the light so intently that when I look down to the ground, I see spots. It's as if the red spots are marking my way like taxiway lights for airplanes. I feel confused with a sense of knowing that I should follow the pathway lights. They're not spots from staring at the light. They are lighting my path. My voice tells me, follow the path, follow the lights. I'm filled with enough energy to begin my journey dragging my 300-pound shoes along the floor of this cave through the unknown. Go. I keep telling myself. Take one more step. You can do it. Go.

My will is strong, but my pace is that of a snail. I follow the pathway lights, inch by inch. My hand drags the side of the cave, feeling every crack and hole as I move along. My journey is excruciatingly slow, and I stop for a moment. The texture of the cave wall has gone from bumpy and damp to smooth like a big thick piece of glass. I lean against the glass with both hands as a light on the other side glows faintly.

I peer through the glass as the light illuminates my wife, Dawn.

She's talking to me, and all I can see is the back of my head. She's giving me a verbal bath of anger and frustration. Her emotions are running high as she screams at me. "Why are you so emotionless? I don't hear any answers. Where are your emotions? You have nothing! How does anybody go through life with no emotions? Where's the passion? Look at you, you can't even answer me. I say one thing, and you shut down. Why? Don't you care? Don't you love me? I'm so amazed that you can sit there and not say a word! I can't live like this! Can you live like this? Do you want to live like this? You'd live like this while the house burns down. You'd be all chill and break out marshmallows. Don't you care? Jesus. I've been asking you this for a long time. Do you care? I keep saying, I can't handle the shut downs. You're like a big block of ice. You ice me, like my dad did when I was a kid. Can't you say something? Can't you get mad?"

I watch myself stand up and walk across the room to her and try to hug her. She wants no part and rejects the hug with a shove. She screams. "West! I don't want this anymore! I don't want you anymore! I don't want this lifeless, emotionless marriage anymore! I'm not pretending anymore. I'm done!"

I watch myself stand there lifeless with my shoulders slumped forward with defeat exuding from my being. I bang on the window and scream at myself. Do something! Do Something! I bang on the glass as the light in the room fades to black. And just like that, I can't see anything. I'm left standing there all alone in a dark pit of nothingness. My stomach aches with the pain of silence and darkness. Rage and anger boil within the pit of my being. I scream from the abyss of my gut. FUCK! The pant of my breath is uncontrollable. I can't get a hold of myself as I rage out in the darkness of the cave.

The little red lights on the floor fade up slowly as I watch them illuminate a path. I have nowhere to go and one choice to make. I follow the pathway of lights. The concrete blocks feel heavier. The journey feels impossible. My mind races with the thoughts of being a complete loser. I am a fucking loser. I wanna run. I wanna jump. I wanna swim. Perfect. If I jumped into a pool, I would sink to the bottom, and this shit would be over. One thought consumes me. Where's the fucking pool? Send me to the bottom and put me out of my misery.

The red lights form a circle around me and begin to flash faster and faster. I'm frozen within the circle and enamored by the lights. The red ones glow solid as the lights behind a pane of glass fade up. I can't believe my eyes. There stands my beautiful mom and myself as a six-year-old, baking cookies. I'm rolling out cookie dough with a big wooden rolling pin as the sound of Christmas music fills the room. My mom is humming Here Comes Santa Claus. I'm pressing a metal cookie cutter into the rolled dough and creating Christmas tree shapes. The red and green sprinkles fall from my hand like fairy dust over the dough. The table is covered with hundreds of freshly baked cookies. The sprinkles pour from my hand as if it's limitless. The mix of red and green sprinkles mesmerizes me. The moment is calm and serene.

Then, the slamming of the front door shifts the energy to dark and negative. I yell out, "Daddy, we made Christmas cookies." My drunken dad stumbles into the kitchen. The stench of alcohol and cheap perfume radiates from his body like a car that's overheating.

Mom immediately asks him, "Are you drunk?"

He shakes his head while Mom's eyes zero in on the red lipstick all over his face and neck. She reaches for the lipstick, but he bats her hand away.

"Dad! Dad, look at all the cookies we made. We made so many."

He ignores me and screams at my mom. His fuse has been lit. The bomb is set to go off at any moment.

"Fuck you!" he screams, his entire body filled with anger and puffed up like a marshmallow.

His face turns bright red and morphs to a round basketball shape, and he appears be blowing up from the inside out. He looks like a Macy's day float getting ready for take off. Then, he takes off on an anger-filled belligerent rant.

He rages at my mom with no regard to who or what is in his way. I feel helpless, clueless and beyond scared.

"You fucking cunt! You're a fucking cunt! And you got your little fucking cunt helper! What are you teaching him? To be a little faggot? Look at the little Suzie fucking homemakers. We'll change his name to Suzie fucking cookie maker. He can make cookies for his boyfriend someday. Fucking fag! They can put icing on each other's dicks and lick it off. A little dick-licking cunt is what you're raising. Making fucking cookies. How fucking sweet."

His ballooned body lumbers toward my mom and corners her against the cabinets. He shoves her hard with both fists and then turns and walks to the table filled with cookies.

She doesn't wince. She is strong and fierce. "You're such a big man! What a big man you are. Screaming at a little boy." He stands over the cookies, glaring. I think he's trying to count them, so I scream out, "There's eight dozen."

He picks up a handful and crams them in his mouth like a grizzly bear, crumbs and spit flying as he shoves them in. I don't think he chews a single one. It is a hostile takeover of our cookies and kitchen. I watch the vein on the side of his head pop out like a raging river. A brief moment of silence fills the room.

"They're good, right?" I ask him.

His face whips toward mine, and he spits all the cookies into my face. I'm hit with spit, dough, and anger.

"They taste like shit! Who the fuck would ever eat such disgusting little turd patties?"

"My family," my mom mutters. "They're for Christmas dinner at my mom's house."

"All of these?" He waves his hand over the cookies like a magician getting ready to perform his next trick. "What about my family? Are you too good for my family? Do they embarrass you?"

"Please stop," Mom says with such calmness that there's a peaceful shift in the energy as his eyes filled with tears.

I truly think he's going to apologize. But no. The tears are like gasoline on a fire. The tears flow as the rage goes up in flames like a wildfire. I observe this man who is supposed to be my father turn non-human. I watch as anger oozes from his soul and spews like a fire hose all over my mom and me. In a split-second, cookies and crumbs fly through the air along with everything on the table. The human volcano has erupted, and we are in his path. He goes from the table to my mom in an instant, shoves her into the wall like a linebacker, and smashes her face against the cabinet. The angry bear within him is unleashed and going to town on her, and his beating is ruthless.

"You fucking cunt!" He shouts. "You think you're better than me? You're nothing more than a cunt! I'm the fucking man of this house. I fucking run this house! Who the fuck said you could make all these goddamn cookies? Who? You wasted all my hard-earned money, you fucking cunt!"

I watch myself as a little boy scream out with bravery, "She works too! And we worked hard to make the cookies."

He shoves the little boy into the wall with a mighty blow. Then he lunges forward and pounces like a lion on it's kill.

My mom leaps from the floor like a crazy monkey and attacks him. She manages to divert his attention but pays the price as he strikes her in the face. He punches until her nose spews blood and her eyes are black and blue. He is so wound up that his anger and the punches cannot stop.

He moves from her face to her body, cranking his fist into her ribs like a prized boxer. I am six years old and have to summon the warrior within. On the counter, I spy a big wooden block, housing a bunch of big knives. I pull a knife from the block like a warrior with his sword. The handle fits my hand perfectly. I am empowered, and with all my might, I scream, "Stop! Stop!"

The madman spins around and finds me standing there with a huge knife, not about to back down. I've had enough. My mom does not deserve this.

I look him dead in the eyes and say, "I'll fucking kill you! Leave her alone!"

He stares at me with uncertainty and it's do or die.

With a calmness in my voice I barely recognize, I tell him one more time, "I'll kill you."

It works. He storms out of the kitchen with a wave of anger following in his wake. He punches the TV with such force that he breaks the screen. Spider web cracks fill the glass, along with a trickle of blood from his hand.

My mom pulls herself from the ground and cleans up the mess. I stand there, holding the knife as adrenaline rushes through my tiny body, and I wonder what the repercussions will be. I stand there, wanting a hug, wanting someone to make it better wanting comfort. All my mom can do is clean the kitchen.

Now I watch me as a child. I try to step forward, but the weights on my feet hold me back. Mortified by what I just watched, I want to give the little boy a hug, and my anger escalates. I'm stuck.

The cave goes completely dark as the energy of anger swirls in my body. I'm consumed by it. The blackness of the cave wraps me like a blanket with no comfort, and the ringing in my head is louder than the silence of the cave. A coldness flows through the air as I continue my journey toward a faint light. It flutters off and on with a consistent white color. I drag my concrete feet inch by inch. My brain screams for me to take the blocks off, but my body won't even allow me to bend over. The sensation is so off the charts. The struggle feels real but stupid. It doesn't make sense. The voice in my head keeps telling me to focus on the light and keep walking toward it. My speed isn't important, but my focus is.

"Think about all the great things that will happen when you reach the light," the voice says.

Occasionally, red lights would ignite from the floor and disrupt my focus on the white one. A faint red glow appears in the cracks of the floor. I follow it, and the crack from the floor leads to a bigger crack in the wall of the cave just big enough for me to peer through.

I see my eleven-year-old self, standing in the bathroom, washing his hands repeatedly. He's looking into the mirror, and I can hear his thoughts. From the mirror, I can see my dad sitting at the dining table. My younger self's thoughts are loud.

"I hate eating with this motherfucker. I hate him. I want to eat in peace. How did I get this guy as a father? He eats like a ravenous rescue dog."

My dad turns from the table to the bathroom and shouts, "Come on West. It's Thanksgiving."

My mom carries a bowl of mashed potatoes to the table and softly calls me.

"West, dinner is ready."

I can't stall any longer. My stomach churns with anxiety, and I wonder if we can actually make it through a dinner. I don't know what to talk about. I'm wondering if he's really my dad.

"I'm coming," I shout and slowly drift into the dining room, but my walk is a little awkward due to my recent growth spurt. My clumsiness is quite evident, and I don't want to be there with my dad. I trip over the multi-colored throw rug and stumble into the table. I feel like the moment should be funny, but my dad doesn't laugh.

"You're like one big goofy, faggot giraffe," he says. "What the fuck? Can't you walk in and sit down?"

I have no response. I merely want this day to be over. I'm so filled with hate and anger toward this beast that calls me son.

Thoughts rage in my head. I want to shoot him, want him dead.

I must have been standing beside the table for too long because he smacks me in the chest and scares the crap out of me.

"Sit down, fag."

The thump in the chest startles me and makes me scream out with a shrill. I grab my chest where he hit me. His laughter isn't funny.

"Ah did I hurt the little pussy? God, I never knew I would have such a little pussy for a son."

I sit down in my chair with so much intensity raging through my body that I feel as if I'm in an out-of-body experience.

He keeps spewing his words of hatred.

"When are you going to become a man?"

"I don't know," I tell him. "I'm eleven."

He leans back in his chair like he is the president of the world. And then he asks me. "You want to know how you know you're a man, a real man? Not one of those pussy men who do dishes and cook. I'm talking about a real man. I'm gonna tell you. It's a simple."

Nothing is simple with this asshole, I think. The only thing simple would be him leaving. I can't fathom what his advice is going to be and brace myself for the words that will spew from his mouth.

He becomes animated with his hand gestures as if he is preaching to the church.

"West, when you're ready to be a man, you step out into the garage, walk up to the work bench, clean off a nice little spot for yourself, pull your pecker out, and place it on the bench, and give it a good smack with a hammer."

My mom lets out a gasp.

He turns to her, "Shut up cunt."

I sit there in disbelief. Does he really think I'm that stupid. I'll remain a boy for the rest of my life if that's the key to manhood.

"Are you seriously telling him to do something so stupid?" My mom demands.

Silence immerses the moment.

"Cunt. Did you just call me stupid?" The rage in my father begins to build and is boiling fast.

I stare at my plate, hoping that we can get through the dinner without an outburst.

"West, Are you ready to go in the garage?"

I can't believe that this is our family conversation, and it is teetering on the verge of an eruption. How is this possible? My self-esteem is riding in the gutter, but my brain does function, and I find the courage to answer him.

"I'm not stupid enough to be a man."

Okay, that's twice that the word stupid has been directed at my dad. His face contorts and stretches as if he is a cartoon. The anger within him comes to a full boil. My mom used the word stupid, and now, so have I. We've crossed the line, and there's no going back. I truly think he believes his manly advice is valid. Perhaps he did it with his dad, but I'm not going to. I'm eleven years old, and my dad has given me the key to life—hit my dick with a hammer. Seriously, who's ignorant enough to believe this crap?

The steam pours from his head, and his face turns bright red. And with one big swipe, he wiped our entire meal onto the floor. Thanksgiving dinner is officially over. He stands up like a neanderthal, grabs his glass of tea, assesses the damage, and throws what remains of his tea on Mom and me.

"You two just ruined our dinner," he says. "Clean it up, cunt, and get your little daughter to help you." And away he goes.

I peer through the crack of the cave and watch my mom and me as a little boy. I have difficulty watching them clean up the broken dishes and wipe the food from the floor. I want to help them and feel the rush of tears flowing down my cheeks as my anger percolates. The cave goes black.

I scan the area for any light that could lead me out of the darkness. As I turn to my right, I can see the faint light of hope off in the distance. The distance feels completely unobtainable, but I have no other options. Once again, I began my journey with the weight of my feet dragging and screeching on the cave floor. The burn in my legs is excruciating, and my thoughts want nothing more than to give up. I need help. I want help.

The voice in my head screams at me, "Stop being a pussy!"

My dad's words echo from the belly of my soul. "You're a pussy."

I'm not going to stop and know I have to push hard. I fixate my sights on the faint light and focus all my energy on taking one step at a time. I repeat over and over, take one step. The thought of taking thousands of steps is overwhelming, but I know I can take one step. I drag my heavy legs, one step at a time, for what feels like eternity and come to a glowing body of water.

The turquoise water is dimly lit from below, and far to the other side, is my beacon of hope. I stand at the water's edge drenched in defeat as I ponder how I will cross this body of liquid with concrete feet. How can I free myself from the dark cave I've been entrapped in?

Deep from the abyss of my gut, I scream out, "I need help!"

The turquoise water fades to a deep, pure blackness. On the far side of the lake, the lights illuminated a scene of me at thirteen.

I'm sleeping in my bed. The room goes from darkness to being lit up as a car pulls into the driveway. The room returns to darkness as I hear the sound of a car door shut, and heavy, stumbling foot steps march to the front door. I sit up in bed. This isn't the first time my dad has come in the middle of the night since my mom divorced him. I know tonight will be the last time he invades our home, our space, our energy, our lives.

I jump out of bed as I hear the front door being kicked open. Drunk and raging, Dad enters the house with a mighty roar as if he's battling an army. I hear the soft footsteps of my mom racing down the hallway. All 110 pounds of her leap at him and try to take him down. She bounces off him and lands on the floor.

"You got your divorce and all my money!" He bellows. "I want my house! You're not getting my house!"

He kicks her in the stomach with his boot, and the look on her face as she gasps for air sends courage piercing through my body. We've been through enough. I reach under my mattress and pulled out my Smith and Wesson 45 that my uncle gave me. Tonight will be the last fucking night of this motherfucker. I don't need to put my dick on a workbench and smack it with a hammer to be a man. Instead, I'm going to stand up to a tyrant. I load a round into the chamber, it's game on. I race out of my room ready to rock and roll. AC/DC Hells Bells fill my head. I'm charged, not backing down. I've already killed this fucker a thousand times in my fantasy.

I'm ready.

I stand before the man I call Dad with nothing more than my underwear on with my 45 pointed directly at his heart.

Calmly, I say, "Stop."

He pulls his leg back to kick my mother one more time.

Again, I say with utter calmness, "Stop."

Our eyes locked as he tries to reach for the gun. My mom rolls away and slowly stands up, not about to show the pain I know she feels.

He holds out his hand, "Can you give me the gun, son?"

For the first time in my life, I'm sure of myself, solid. I'm a man protecting the one person in my life. This moment is the most important time of my life. I keep my calm, keep my clarity and my focus. I know this motherfucker. I know everything about him. I study his face as he begins to boil.

I stand there in my concrete boots watching my thirteen-year-old self about to shoot my dad. It's gut wrenching, and I need to help. My only choice is to jump into the water and get to my younger self. I jump, weights on my feet, and straight to the bottom I go, screaming in my mind, with every cell of my body.

"Please help me!"

I hit the bottom and struggle to get the weights off my feet. My body moves in a frantic motion as I panic to remove the weights.

"Help!"

The water churns around me as I struggle fiercely, and at that moment, I don't quit. I accept that I truly need help. The water clears, and a calmness overtakes my body as Charlie appears, and I feel the relief in my soul.

"West, reach down and let the weights go." He can talk under water with such clarity.

"I can't," I say. "They're stuck."

"West, you can do it. It's all in your mind. Trust me."

The pain and burning in my lungs force me to focus and listen to him. I reach down to the buckle, and just like that, the weights release. I was free!

Charlie grabs me by the shoulders. "Go free yourself, West. You can do it. Remember, something old must die before something new can begin."

I swim to the top like a dolphin and catapult myself from the water, landing next to my thirteen-year-old self. He looks at me with a hint of fear in his eyes. I reassured him it will be okay.

"I'm here to help you," I tell him, and he hands me the gun. I point it at my dad. I need answers from the old man. I want him to explain.

"Why did you abuse me and my mom?" I demand. "Why?"

He stares at the grown-up and breaks down. His tears are uncontrollable. The bottom of abuse has been reached.

"I didn't know how to be any different," he says. "I used the tools that were passed down to me from my father, and I was too embarrassed to ask for help. I wanted to be happy. I wanted to be a good dad. I'm sorry."

I stare at a broken man and say, "I accept your words, but I can't forgive your actions." Then, I pull the trigger.

The bullet spirals from the barrel in slow motion as I watch it fly through the air and pierce him in the heart. The anger and rage are over. I can move forward in peace, or so I think.

I turn to hug the little boy, but he's gone. I spin desperately in a circle, frantically searching for him. Now, as I stand there alone, still trapped within the cave, there is a pack on my back. The pack is heavy as if I am carrying a year's supply of food for camping. In an odd kind of way, I don't mind the weight. It has a since of calmness to it.

I'm compelled to walk toward a beam of light cascading through a crack in the cave. I crawl over rocks and boulders and make my way to it. Then, I stand staring at all the light shining through the crack and watch the thick dust particles swirl about. I am simply mesmerized. The particles of dust speed up with time as I gaze at them, and letters form and spell out, "Forgiveness."

I reach into the dust and grab the word as if I can put it into my pocket, but hard as I try, I can't grasp it. The light disappears, and there stands Charlie.

"West," he calls to me. "You're up, Lad." I have no clue what he's talking about. He reaches his hand out. "West, hand me your backpack." He takes the pack and shoves it through a hole in the cave.

Then, he motions for me to crawl through the hole. The light coming through it is ultra-bright and blinding. I squeeze through and pop out the other side to a loud speaker announcing my name.

"Please give a big round of applause for West Falia."

The audience roars with applause as Charlie slips the backpack on to my back. The intensity of the crowd fills the room, and I struggle to carry the pack.

I look at Charlie and demand, "Why is this thing so heavy? How am I supposed to go on stage with this heavy-ass pack? I need a mule."

"Have you ever looked in your backpack?" Charlie asks.

I'm totally confused by his question. "Of course, I have. Why would I carry it around if I never looked inside?"

Charlie maintains his calm expression. "It appears to me that you have not looked in your backpack, nor have you taken an inventory."

"An inventory?" I ask. "What am I, a Wal-Mart employee?"

Charlie walks behind me and pulls something from the pack. Wow. It feels so much lighter.

I look across the stage and see Dawn, my ex-wife, standing in a single ray of light. The darkness surrounds her as if she's frozen in time.

"Can you feel the weight I've lifted from your shoulders?" Charlie asks.

I nod my head yes.

Charlie says, "The weight is forgiveness. I want you to walk over to your ex-wife and tell her you forgive her."

Without hesitation, I respond, "Fuck that."

And without hesitation, Charlie drops the weight back in the pack, and the light surrounding my ex-wife goes black. She's gone.

Charlie asks, "Do you want to feel love?"

"I'd like to have love tattooed on my knuckles and punch her in the face," I reply.

Then, I feel a pain in my hand and look to see that Love has been tattooed on my knuckles. Charlie reaches into my pack and pulls out another heavy object.

"It feels lighter?" He asks, and I nod.

The sound of a spotlight pops on and illuminates my dad. Bright white light cascades around him.

"West. You want to forgive him?" Charlie asks.

"Fuck no! I hate that motherfucker."

The immediate clicking sound of the spotlight turning off fills the room. The weight of my backpack pulls me to the ground.

"Do you like carrying around all the extra baggage?" Charlie asks.

"Apparently, I do, Charlie," I tell him. "Apparently, I do."

4
SELF-DESTRUCTION

"In this moment I shall destroy or call for courage"

I'm lying flat on the floor in the most awkward position while staring up at the ceiling. A golden light cuts through the cold winter air on the front porch. I'm merely a lifeless mat placed in front of the door. Christmas lights line the front and flash red, green and white. A large wreath laced with pinecones, candy canes, and small trumpets hangs from the front door.

I'm completely lifeless because my body has melded into the form of a doormat. People are stepping on me, walking over me, wiping their shoes on me before entering the house. I know I don't want to be here, but I can't summon the energy to get up. The sound of festive Christmas music fills the air, giving the illusion that all is joyous. I have no joy. I have no happiness. I have no peace. I'm this lifeless rectangular piece of shit mat who's unable to move and basically licks the bottom of everyone's shoes. And that depends how you look at the situation.

The front door opens with Dawn and my two kids walking onto the front porch.

Emma asks, "Where's dad?"

Dawn answers, "I don't know."

The kids race into the yard as the snow falls like cotton balls falling from the sky. I hear the words coming from my mouth, but no one else does.

"I'm right here!"

Here I am at the foot of the door with no voice, no backbone, nothing. I'm a doormat. Dawn yells out to the kids, "Be sure to wipe your feet before you come into the house."

I feel paralyzed as the cold breeze blows across me. I want to get up and play. I want to be a part of their lives and help build a snowman. I have no control of my situation. I am reduced to being an observer, or so I think. If I could push a button and disintegrate my current situation, I would. The kids race in from the yard and stomp their feet on the mat. All the lights on the porch go to black.

I'm standing here on top of a bridge surrounded by a billion stars. A sliver of moon and a gentle breeze try to penetrate my soul. One single tear drops from my cheek. I watch as the tear rolls off my cheek and floats through the air. It falls in slow motion while contorting in many different directions as it drops through the cold, dark night. Within the tear, I can see sadness, anger, loneliness, rage, disappointment, and fear. All the emotions are encapsulated within the teardrop. It is at peace floating through the universe as though there is a purpose to it's journey. Maybe its purpose is to carry away all the pain and sadness. The pain of losing my children. The pain of my childhood. The pain of my failed marriage. There it is, right in front of me, floating away in one teardrop across the cold night sky.

I can't see myself connected to the drop. I feel myself wanting to be like it though, falling to my death because that's what the teardrop is doing. It's slowly falling to its death. Because as peaceful as the tear looks, it is on a path to death. There's no way it can stay suspended in mid-air forever. The tear will eventually go splat on the pavement. That will be the death of my fear, anxiety, depression, sadness, and loneliness. Although I watch it disappear, my emotions do not subside. My body still houses all these emotions. I am a dam, waiting to burst.

How does a soul store this plethora of sadness? And why? I scan my arm as if to find an on/off switch. There are deep black words written on my hands. My knuckles have been tattooed with the words, "Fuck Life."

A bold loud voice screams in my head, "FUCK LIFE!" I hold my hands out in front of me as far as I can stretch them out and stare at them. They feel separate from me. They look like someone else's hands, but nobody else is around. I have reached the bottom but am standing at the top of the bridge.

I read the words as the voice in my brain repeats loudly, "Fuck life, fuck life, fuck life, fuck life, fuck life." There I stand so high up that you can't see the bottom of darkness, nor can you hear a sound. Only the stars give me a minuscule of comfort, but it isn't much, and I don't care. The chant continues in my head, "Fuck life, fuck life, fuck life." It has rhythm, that chant, but no soul, and it is quite intoxicating. I don't want to turn it off. The annoying, repetitive chant has put me into a state of bliss. I am accepting my destiny. I am accepting that my life has no purpose. I am accepting my life is complete and utter shit. I am accepting death or possibly the death of my emotions. I know it is time to kill these motherfuckers.

I want these haunting emotions to die.

Death to loneliness. Death to anger. Death to sadness. Death to depression. Death to it all. Fuck you, God! Fuck you! And just like that, I jump.

I leap off the bridge like there is no tomorrow. I scream from the depth of my soul, "Fuck Life! Fuck You!"

There I am suspended in time, suspended in the cool black air. Darkness engulfs my body as the stars surround me to keep me safe. I'm not falling. No, I'm a part of the universe, suspended in darkness while staring at the bridge.

My body feels lifeless and weightless as if I have control, but I really don't. I observe myself surrounded in darkness with the feeling that something or someone has control of my destiny. The screams of "fuck life" have subsided in my head, and I didn't know what to do, who to talk to. I don't even know what to ask.

For a brief moment, I know I have a body, but that's all I know. And in an instant, the sun rises over the ridge, exposing a bridge that stretches from one mountain peak to another with huge ocean waves crashing far, far below. The piercing golden light consumes my body, and just like that, I am gone.

The bright light makes a huge attempt to penetrate my squinted eyes. I squeeze my eye lids tighter to keep it out. In the background, I can hear the consistent hum of a motor. The pain in my face that feels like a million needles attempting to penetrate my skin. I reach for a bottle of whiskey on the ground. The sunspots in my eyes make it hard to see. The tattoo artist stops briefly, grabs the whiskey bottle by the neck and takes a big draw as if it's water. He hands it to a piercing artist who's putting rods in my ears. She takes a big drink like a sailor and then passes me the bottle. I finish the bottle off like there's no tomorrow. The ear piercer is fumbling with my ear lobe.

When she sees that half of it is gone, she asks, "What happened?" The lights in the tattoo shop dim, and a projector shoots a moving image onto the wall. My childhood memory comes to life.

I'm eight years old, playing on the floor with my Hot Wheels track. I'm racing cars down a long, orange track that suspends from a tall chair and across the floor. In the background, I can hear my mom and dad arguing in the kitchen. My dad's voice is getting louder and louder. He's talking about my hair.

"He looks like a little queer with that hair."

I keep racing my cars and ignore the verbiage spewing from his mouth. I don't really know what queer means.

My mom fires back, "He's eight years old. Who cares about his hair?"

My dad is getting louder. "I care. That's who cares. I don't want my boy growing up to be a little faggot."

I hear the sound of my mom crashing to the ground and feel the strong grasp as my father whisks me up.

He barks out, "We're getting your hair cut." And away we go.

There I am, sitting in the barber chair with the black apron tied around my neck, staring into the mirror watching my long, white hair falling to my shoulders as the barber shaves my head. I can see my dad in the mirror, watching so proudly as if I were winning a sporting event. I think he feels a huge sense of accomplishment, but I feel like a little boy who is forced to become a man.

I stare at myself and realize I looked older. My hair is prickly on top like a peach. I don't look like me. The roar of the electric trimmer buzzes louder and louder. My hair floats to the ground like feathers. There is no going back. The decision was purely made by one big asshole, my dad. I keep asking myself, who is this guy? I am so deep in thought that I can barely hear the electric trimmer. My deep thought comes to an abrupt end as pain erupts from my ear.

The barber lost his concentration and sliced off my earlobe. My pure white T-shirt bleeds bright red, and tears swell in my eyes as the pain shoots through my body.

My dad races to my side.

"Don't you fucking cry! You hear me? Don't you fucking cry!" I try to choke back the tears. My dad's voice bellows in my head. "Man up, you little fag, Man up."

I try hard not to let the tears flow down my cheeks, but one leaks out as my breath becomes uncontrollable.

I mumble to my dad, "Do you think Mom can get the blood out of my T-shirt?"

He doesn't answer. Instead, he grabs the barber by the neck and throws him across the room, shouting, "I'm not paying for this!"

The grown-up me enters the barbershop to see myself as a kid sitting in the barber chair with that blood-soaked T-shirt. My dad is doing what he thinks is right. He holds the barber by the throat with one hand while he punches him in the gut with the other.

I put my hand on the younger me to offer comfort and support. My dad says, "Take your hand off my kid."

I turn to him, with my face completely covered in tattoos and piercings in my nose and ears. My entire body is covered in tattoos from head to toe.

Then, I say in a calm voice, "The boy needs support or simply a hug."

My dad gives the barber one last punch to the gut and turns his complete attention to me.

"What he doesn't need is a hug from some faggot, freak-looking asshole like you. Who the fuck tattoos FUCK LIFE on their forehead?" I am not backing down from this asshole. This tyrant has to be dealt with. He looks me dead in the eyes. "I'm going to tell you one more time to take your hand off my kid."

I need to stand up to him. He throws a punch so fast and fierce that although I try with all my might to fight back, I can't. I have nothing.

He punches me in the face, but I don't feel the pain. My face is numb to his anger. He punches me again, and I stumble backward, tripping over a small round table. I stand up as if it didn't faze me.

Then, I walk back to the boy and place my hand on his shoulder. I stay there to give the boy strength, security, and love. My dad doesn't say a word; he didn't have to. His face is filled with rage and anger that spews from his fists. He smashes me in the face again. I fly back and land in a chair.

I can feel blood running down my face and dripping from my jaw onto my clothing and the floor. I'm not scared. I am numb to this asshole. The numbness fills my body as I look at this man who called himself my dad.

I can see myself in a mirror across the shop. I truly looked horrifying with my "FUCK LIFE" tattoo and blood-covered face. I don't care. I am happy to take the hit for the boy. I wanted him to know I am here for him, that someone will stand up for him.

I pull myself to my feet and walk to the boy's side again. I reach out and put my hand on his shoulder.

My dad looks at me and says, "You are one stupid motherfucker."

"I'm your son," I say, and pat the boy on the shoulder. "Go ahead. Beat the fuck out of me. You can't hurt me anymore than you already have." I feel the rage stir within my soul. The anger within me wants to boil. "Come on, Dad! Hit me! You're so fucking tough. Hit me, Dad! You think a punch to the face is going to matter? My life is utter shit! Nothing matters. You know what matters to me?"

His eyes pierce mine, and he says, "Take your hand off my fucking kid."

I try with all my strength to lift my hand and wrap my arms around that little boy. I stare into the boy's soul and use all my might to tell him I love him.

But I can't speak to him. Nothing comes out. I can't hug him. I have nothing for him except a hand on his shoulder.

I stare at my dad and look deep within his soul. BAM! He rocks me in the face again and again and again. He hits me so many times I lose count. My thoughts tell me the punches should hurt. No, his mighty fist can't hurt me. The numbness in my body is at maximum capacity. A man's fist can't penetrate it.

I laugh at my dad, loud and from the gut. The laughter is my pain. The pain isn't mine. It belongs to the little boy in the chair. He never moves. He never speaks. He sits in silence as a witness to a brutal ass beating and never says a word. He is numb, a boulder in the hot desert sun. He sits there in fear, knowing the ass kicking could have been him.

I watch as he consumes the fear without realizing it. I watch my little boy frozen in fear. It has a color as it swirls around him in shades of gray and black. He has no idea that the fear is circling his body and penetrating his soul. He has become the fear. I observe in sadness, but my own numbness blocks any emotion. I want to pull the fear from the child, but I don't know how. I am merely an observer who cannot help. I feel beyond worthless as blood runs down my face. I can't even find the strength to get up.

"Big Pussy is what you should tattoo across your forehead. What does Fuck Life mean? All you are is one big pussy."

He walks to the boy and grabs him by the arm.

"Hey Dad," I shout. "What are you?"

He doesn't miss a beat and yells back, "I'm a goddamn man. Only the fit survive, you fucking pussy." And then, he is out the door.

I did nothing to help the boy. If anything, I made it worse for him. Why couldn't I at least lift my hands to give him a hug. All I wanted to do was hug him. I allowed this fucking tyrant to rob me of a hug. It's as if I can see what to do, but I can't feel it.

The familiar sound of Charlie's motorcycle screeches to a stop outside the barbershop.

He enters the building with confidence, poise, and grace and flashes me a look of comfort and love.

He speaks with elegance, asking "Do you want a ride, kid?"

I can't find the strength to answer, so I shake my head. Every cell in my body screams yes, but my head swivels from side to side. Charlie doesn't ask a second time. He is gone. The sound of his motorcycle roars in the distance.

I stand in the street undecided which way to walk. The street feels dark and lonely. I am alone as a whisper of light illuminates my surroundings. I walk through the silence of the night with the sound of my foot steps and my shoes echoing in my head. I stop for a moment to see if I can hear myself breathing. Nothing. I can't hear a thing. My walk is hard and forceful with each step resonating through my body. My choice of direction is dictated by the buildings. The building and objects in my path force my direction along the sidewalk and I have no choice but to follow the path that is guiding me. I stretch out my arms wide and can feel the bricks and mortar with my fingertips.

The walk seems to last forever. My index finger on both hands follow the mortar crack within each brick. It is smooth and rough at the same time. Every once in a while, I feel a big chunk, and my hand rolls right over it. The chunks feel strong, and I gain a sense of strength from them, as if I am part of the walls I allowed to guide me in a slow, mythical way. There is a sense of comfort in allowing them to guide me. All I have to do is walk.

It's not so easy though. I walk into a dead end. The walls have closed in on me. I reach out with my hands and lean on the wall in front of me. I don't feel trapped, but I need to push through, to push the wall. I lean into it with all my weight and use all the leverage of my body and strength in my legs to push. The wall doesn't budge.

The sound of one big water drop going splat on the ground

makes me turn around, and I see two doors that look identical. Each has a tag attached. The door on the right has a tag that reads, LOVE. The door on the left has one that reads, SELF-DESTRUCTION.

I curl my hand into a fist and knock on the door of love. It has a big golden lock that's quite soothing to the eye. I reach out for the knob and grasp it. Then, I turn the knob and gently push on the door. It's solid, though, and my attempt to open it is quite weak. The door doesn't budge. I lean my head against it and see the beautifully sculpted wood that appears to be alive and breathtaking. The wood grain is moving, and breathing, it's mesmerizing. Everything about this door is beautiful and intoxicating. Even the golden lock is breathing with movement. I ask myself, "Where's the key?" I need a key. I caress my hands across the lock, seeking.

The voice in my head is on repeat. "You don't have the key. You don't deserve the key. You are not worthy of the key."

I turn to the other door with its dull, gray finish. It's made from cold, hard steel, which has formed rust in various spots, but its appearance gives the illusion of strength. In the center of the door, a red light is elongated and shaped like a half-moon. It's just big enough for me to place my thumb in it.

I stare at it and, without making a conscious decision, I put my thumb in the half moon. I press my thumb firmly into the light. A loud latch sound echoes in the night. The lock disengages with a loud mechanical boom, and the door opens with ease.

I walk in as if I have been there a million times. Am I home? No. But close enough. The smell of rubber mats and fermented alcohol laced with a stained nicotine ceiling goes straight into my nose. I stand in a dimly lit bar. It doesn't matter which bar. They all smell the same. They all look the same in the night. They all sound the same regardless if they're country or rock.

The bartender slings bottles of beer and shots of tequila on the bar as people drink non-stop, the smell of cigarettes encases everything. The smoke is thick, but through the fog, I can see a small television hung behind the bar. Evel Knievel is jumping his motorcycle at Cesars Palace.

I sit down at the bar and give a quick wave to the bartender. He's the gatekeeper to the spirits that flow from the glass bottles. I stand with my back to the bar and scan the room. A beautiful blonde appears before me as if she's an angel. She pulls a cigarette from her cleavage and flicks it into my mouth. I whip a silver Zippo lighter from my pocket and flame my cig to life. The blonde disappears as if she were never there.

I turn to the bar and catch the drink the bartender slides to me. It's a highball glass filled with rocks and Stoli. I drink the vodka, and by the time my glass hits the bar, it's magically filled. I take big drags off my cigarette, but the length stays long. I'm able to blow huge smoke rings across the room. One of them floats across the room. My eyes follow the ring as it takes me to a seven-year-old boy playing pool. It's an odd sight to see such a young boy in a place of adults.

It's me with my long, blond curly hair. I'm holding the pool cue and leaning on the table with my chest. A large ornate gold key hangs from my neck by a red piece of yarn that has faded pink. I watch as the boy attempts a shot but misses. Flanking the boy are two blonde, big-titted women with cigarettes hanging from their lips and bright red lipstick. They're putting their tits on his head and running their hands through his wispy hair. If he were fourteen, this experience would be all time, but for a boy who's seven. He's scared. I scan the bar for my dad.

He emerges from the bathroom and has clearly been doing cocaine and having sex. He snorts extremely loud as if he's vacuumed up all the blow in Colombia. Then, he adjusts his jeans and buckles his belt to show everyone how manly he is by having sex in a bar. A dark-haired girl emerges from the shadows behind him, giggling and running her hands on his chest. She adjusts her bra to tuck in her big boobs while smacking on a piece of Hubba Bubba grape-flavored gum.

My dad shouts, "Next!" And the bar erupts with laughter.

He walks to the pool table and pulls a huge wad of one-hundred-dollar bills from his pocket. He counts out ten of them and lays them on the table. "Who wants to play me and my boy? One game. One thousand dollars." He blurts it out so loud with his big barrel chest sticking out. He struts around the table like he's a king, hoists his beer to his mouth, and chugs it down.

The two girls with big boobs step up to the pool table with their pool cues.

"We don't have cash," one of them says. "But we can offer our services."

My dad doesn't hesitate to answer, "Rack them."

I watch the little boy stand beside the pool table. He's so nervous that he accidentally bites into the cube of chalk.

Dad snaps his fingers at him. "Let's go. Pay attention. We got big money on this. Rack the balls, boy."

The little boy is slow to put the balls in the rack, and my dad is so high he has no patience. He shoves the little boy out of the way and racks the balls himself. The game is on. The girls make a couple of balls. Dad drains a couple of balls. The little boy can't make a shot. He's too nervous. The girls make a couple more balls. Dad sinks two more balls. The young boy walks around the table, looking for a shot.

I watch him from my barstool. I want to help him. I want to go over there and whisk him up and get him out of this place. I can't even help myself. All I can do is sit here and drink, glass after glass of alcohol. My ass is glued to the stool. I'm not going anywhere.

My dad's patience is nil. He screams out at the boy, "Why in the fuck would you shoot that shot? Do you see how much money Daddy has on the table? I would like to win this game. Do you see these two gorgeous hotties we're playing? We win, and we get our dicks sucked. Right? You can goto school tomorrow and tell all the kids you got your wanker sucked.

"My boy will be a stud at school."

The little boy stares down at the floor. He doesn't understand what his dad is saying. All he knows is that he's embarrassed.

The awkward moment of silence is pierced by the sound of my mom's voice barreling into the bar. She charges across the floor and grabs the boy by the hand. She lets my dad have it.

"How can you bring your child to a bar on a Sunday afternoon? You said you were going to help clean the church."

Dad takes a gulp of beer and wipes his face. He doesn't like being embarrassed by her. He stands erect in attack mode.

"You assumed your church. This is my church with real fucking people. We got holy water with barley and the white goodness from the gods of Bogota. Now, sit down and pull the stick from your ass. West and I have a game to finish. We're having a little father/son bonding time. Once we win, the boy gets his little pee-pee kissed. He won't be a little queer anymore or a momma's boy."

Dad's boiling temper is showing its ugly head. My mom grabs the boy by the hand and tries to leave. Dad shoves her into the pool table.

"A bet is a bet."

The bar is silent as everybody watches and nobody helps. I jump to my feet, but I'm powerless. I fall flat on my face. My consumption of alcohol has taken control. As I lie with my face smashed to the crusty carpet. I can see the short legs of the boy crawl under the pool table and run to his mom. She grabs his hand and heads for the door.

My dad is yelling, "You're raising a little faggot. Fucking Momma's boy. That's all he'll ever be."

The two of them escape darkness and run out the door into the light of Sunday afternoon.

What a piece of shit I am. I couldn't get off the floor to help. I'm lying here as if I don't exist. This is truly a fucked-up situation. Do I care? No. I don't care. I want to care. I'm talking to myself, and no one notices my lame ass lying on the floor. Why would anyone care if I don't? I'm merely a lowlife piece of garbage. You're fucking trash. One big pile of trash. Do us all a favor and stick a gun in your mouth. Just get it over with. The voice in my head is harsh. The voice sounds a lot like my dad's.

I want to end it all. The boy needed me and I couldn't do anything to help. Maybe I should end my toxicity of being a human. I could end the cycle of not showing up for myself. I'm about as low as I can go.

The lights are bright and flashing in my eyes as I stumble down the wet, dark street. My eyes are blurred by the headlights in my eyes. My ears are ringing from the loud obnoxious car honking. I'm lost in the middle of the road, walking aimlessly toward nowhere. The yellow line is my guide as I try my best to walk on it with no balance as the cars zoom past my shoulders on both sides. Large droplets of rain fall through the sky in slow motion. The streetlights illuminate their enormous size. I can see the rain bounce off my nose one drop at a time. There's a semi-soothing effect as they touch my skin. The sting actually feels good. I stare up to the sky and see only a whiteish wall of water falling on my face.

The sound of the rain pounds the roof as lightning and thunder crack in the night sky. The lightning lights my childhood room as I see me as a little boy. I'm hiding under the bed with my tiny, blue security blanket that reeks of bad breath. The lightning illuminates my room and a poster of Roger Decoster coming out of a berm on his Suzuki RM 250. Another crack of thunder and lightning highlights a poster of Evel Knievel jumping buses. The inside of the house feels dark and cold as the thunder booms away. Unfortunately, the thunder is not loud enough to drown out the sound of my parents fighting. I'm walking down a hallway that feels like it goes forever as shouts, and screams come from my mom and dad. The shrill voice of my mom echoes in the hallway. The roar of the thunder muffles a fraction of the noise as I hear the rage in my dad's billowing anger. The fight is intense with furniture being moved and the thud of bodies hitting the floor.

My mom screams out, "You can't hurt me. Nothing you do can hurt me." The thunder roars and the lightning cracks as the intensity of the fight escalates.

The hallway disappears as I stand in my room. I remember this day. I look at my perfectly made bed with the football pillow. The little boy under the bed lay there so stoically. If I didn't know him, I'd say he was fine, but I know him. The storm inside the house and outside rage with a mighty fury that no one could control. The fear I felt as a child that day was not measurable. I felt alone. Fuck I was alone. Whom would I tell? And if I did tell, I'd get the fuck beat out of me.

I watch the little boy move from the bed to the closet. He drags his security blanket in one hand and grabs a pillow from the bed with his other hand. The raging noise from the fight is unbearable. You can hear broken glass, broken dishes, furniture moving, and bodies being beaten.

The little boy crawls into the closet and wraps the pillow around his head while squeezing it tightly. He needs to muffle out the chaos and rage. His only comfort is the small, stinky, blue, crusty security blanket he clutches. I watched him and remembered every single emotion I felt and all the wishes I made that night. I wished for peace. I wished for normalcy. I wished for a brother. I wished my dad would fucking DIE. I wished to escape. I stared at my photos to help my mind escape the hell I was living in. My tiny flashlight lit my collection of photos and magazine cutouts. I stared at my photo of Evel jumping his motorcycle over buses with his white superman suit. He was my hero. I looked at my photos of guys being shot out of barrels at Pipeline. The photos helped me escape the trauma. The photos gave me a place to go. They made you feel like you were there and nobody could take that away.

I stare at a pack of motorcycles racing across the desert with dust consuming everything. They race across land that has no end. I could escape there without being found. I can smell the dust mixed with the sweet smell of two-stroke gas. I can feel my forearms tighten as I twist the throttle without a care in the world. In my mind, I am running triple digits as I race across the sand. I'm not winning. I'm escaping and nobody can catch me. The cool, crisp night air of the desert invigorates me. I am the youngest rider to ever race in the Baja 500. Wow! That's all I can think. I hold the throttle wide open on my 1974 Penton 125 as it drinks gas like a thirsty camel. The moonlit sky lights my way to freedom laced with exhilaration. I am one with this bike. It might as well be my arm or leg. We are inseparable. I can feel the freedom. I can taste the freedom of dirt, gas, and desert air. The energy I felt being among so many great riders is electrifying. I have one speed. I keep her pinned. The rush of speed, wind, and sudden unexpected launches make me feel alive. I am and have never felt this alive. And I am not afraid to die. Living in the existence of my dad was death. My Baja light illuminates the perfect line, and my mind is laser sharp. Nothing can interrupt me. I know all I have to do is twist the throttle, keep my ass just above the seat, and allow my knees to absorb all the shock.

The sound of the wind grows silent as my speed increases. I truly hear nothing except peace. The ride is effortless. It's as if I'm not riding but have become one with the motorcycle, the ground, and desert air. The darkness of the night holds it all together. I want this feeling to last forever. What an amazing moment in time. I'm a part of it, but then, I'm not.

I realize that I love this moment. I love being on my motor-cycle. I love the race. I love the desert. I love the night. I love the air. I love the wind. I love the taste of dirt. I love how alive I am. I feel like a warrior, and nothing or no one can stop me. And then I think, nothing can go wrong. And in that thought, I hear the rage of my dad's voice permeate my thoughts and penetrate my soul. His billowing anger spews at my mom.

I twist the throttle more to drown out his voice. The intensity of the wind magnifies inside my helmet along with the increased whine of RPMs winding in my engine. I've got the throttle pegged while repeating the words, you got to pin it to win it.

The effortless glide of the ride has diminished. I'm feeling every bump, rock, and scrub brush alter my path. My line of attack is not clear. My eyes are filled with water as my dad's voice rages in my head. "The kid is a little mama's boy. He's a little pussy who will always be a little pussy. How's a little pussy going to survive in the world? Tell me, you fucking cunt! I took him to the bar and gave him a taste of what real men do. He had his first taste of whiskey and pussy. What do you think about that, cunt? He got some big titties in his face. And if your cunt ass hadn't come along, he would have dipped his little pecker in some pussy pie. I think he's a little queer cause all he wants to do is hide out in the kitchen with you. He's got to be a man! A real man! A real man! A real man!

The roar of the two stroke gets louder and louder as I lose

control. My dad's disarray of words echoes in my head. His words have permeated my soul. I lose all control of the bike and don't care. My speed is pushed to the limit of no going back. I'm running from the voice in my head but can't seem to outrun it. Although I give it everything I have, I can't create enough speed to drown out his words.

A brown bunny rabbit crosses my path. I fly from the seat and launch over the handlebars, feeling myself sailing in slow motion as my dad's words scream in my head.

"You're not a real man. You're a fucking loser. You queer. You'll never be a real man."

I fly through the air in slow motion with his words on repeat. My thoughts creep in. I hope I die. I don't care. Just die.

A symphony of words battles in my head. The words from my dad intertwine with my own thoughts and stay on repeat. The moment feels like a lifetime.

The glide through the air starts to have an intoxicating effect because I don't care about the outcome. I know the landing will hurt, but it will never match the pain I am harboring. You can't kill someone who is already dead inside.

BAM! I land on the desert floor with a mighty thud and roll forever. The wafts and billow of dust hide my lifeless body as I roll across the sand. The best part is, all my dad's screaming, yelling, and belittling is gone. I can no longer hear that motherfucker. Please let me keep rolling.

I come to a stop. The dust clears and the sky is crystal blue with the taste of saltwater in the air. I sit in the sand on the beach with my surfboard next to me while staring at the waves. A mass of people gathers on the beach to watch the contest taking place at Pipeline on the North Shore. The beach announcer calls my name over the loud PA along with Mark Richards, Sean Thompson, and Gerry Lopez. I'm checking in for my heat and about to go up against the best to have ever ridden Pipe. The announcer gives an intro about me.

"We have West Falia paddling out with the Greats of Pipe. West is the youngest competitor to ever qualify for the Pipe Masters."

The crowd cheer as I watch big gaping barrels reel across the reef and spit like they just ate you for breakfast.

I stare at Gerry Lopez in amazement and can't quite believe I am paddling out with such a legend. He appears so calm and Zen like. I want to be like him. His red Lightning Bolt board twinkles in the sun. I stare at the lightning bolt logo, hoping it will give me magical powers because I know I need all the help I can get. Gerry walks up beside me, carrying his board like a gladiator going into battle. He looks down at my bare board.

"Are you gonna wax your board up?" He asks.

I look at Gerry with all the confidence in the world and say, "I've been training for this day my whole life."

He pats me on the back and hands me a chunk of wax. "Here you go, just in case you actually want to make the drop."

I grab the wax but don't take the time to wax my board. The deck of it is slick, but I don't care.

I tuck my board under my arm and race across the sand to the water's edge. The starting horn blows as I jump into the shore break and pull my board under my body with my arms while stroking myself out to the lineup. The water is ultra-clear and deep blue.

Not one set comes in as I paddle out. The entire ocean goes flat as I look to the horizon and feel I can reach out and touch where the sky meets the ocean. I reach the lineup with dry hair and sit up on my board.

The sun is coming up off my right shoulder, as I can see a sliver of the moon off to the left of me. I stare at the moon briefly and have a split second of clarity as I think, the moon is whole rather you see it as a sliver or as fully lit. I feel this innate energy and guidance from the moon as I observe it doing nothing but what it's supposed to be doing. I feel centered and connected to something that feels so far away. How can that be?

The cheer of the crowd breaks my stare as I turn my focus to the horizon, cup water from the ocean with my hand, and splash myself in the face. The connection to the water seems timeless and makes me feel free. I know I look like a kid, but on the inside, I feel so wise and mature. The water gives me a sense that no matter what, I am good. My body moves with intention and no thought. My brain doesn't say lay down and paddle. I just do it. I paddle into the most perfect wave to roll in—a beautiful bomb that glistens as she stands up with each roll she takes. She appears to be dancing as she rolls toward the shore.

I can see my name written into the face of the wave. This is my wave; it has my name written right across the curling face. I swing my board around and paddle effortlessly. I pop up to my feet land on the deck with such grace. My body is in perfect position as I drop down the face of the wave in slow motion. The deep blue-green water forms the perfect wall for me to make my descent as I grab the rail and lean my back into the glassy face of the wave.

I stall to the perfect pace to allow the entire face to pitch over my body.

I stand up tall and stare in awe out the mouth of this beast. I hear nothing. There is no sound. Time seems to slow down to a beautiful pace that feels somehow dreamlike. The wave is a living, breathing extension of me, and I am an extension of her. She is absolutely beautiful, and she doesn't think about what she needs to do; she just does it.

Like her, I don't think about what I need to do. In this moment, I'm taking in the beauty of a rolling piece of art and feeling so at one with everything around me. There are water, board, and me three entities alive and acting as one. The beauty consumes me, and it's as if I'm meeting myself for the first time. I'm in awe of the sheer power, glow, and size. For this brief moment, I'm in bliss, in love. I'm in love with the feeling of riding the wave, knowing we are one.

I want this moment to last forever, and then the silence becomes engulfed by the explosion of whitewater as a blast of air shoots my ass out of the tube. The joy and excitement jolt through my body and blast my hands up high. It is all feeling. I rejoice in the stoke of riding the wave of my life. I skim to the shoulder, swing my board to the horizon and slide to the deck with my belly. The roar of the crowd feeds my adrenaline as I paddle hard to the lineup.

I want another one. I need another one. I'm pumped, and nothing can get in my way. The energy from the crowd pours into my soul like gas on a fire. I paddle with passion and purpose along with clarity. I hear the announcer call out that I got a 10! A perfect score! If I can get another bomb, I can beat Gerry.

I get back to the line up, and I'm sitting to the inside of all the other surfers. Their backs are to me as I look in amazement that I'm sitting in the lineup with such great surfing icons. Questions arise in my head. Can I really do this? Am I really good enough? I call out to Gerry to let him know that I didn't need wax on my board.

He turns to look at me. I'm waiting for a compliment or an attaboy. His face turns and we look eye to eye. It's not Gerry; it's my dad.

MR turns around, only he's my dad.

Sean turns to me, and he's my dad too.

The voice in my head screams, "What the fuck?"

My amazing, beautiful day with a golden sun and perfect turquoise waves turns dark and stormy within seconds. The black clouds roll in, carrying heavy winds and rain. I sit there alone on my board with the rain pouring on my head and the splash of the ocean slapping me in the face.

My ex-wife paddles next to me.

"See what you created," she says.

"What I created?" I scream back, "You ask for the divorce. You created this fucking mess. Fuck you! Why in the fuck would you paddle out here to say something so stupid?"

She seems so happy with herself, but it's a fake kind of happiness.

"Come on, West. It was the same routine over and over and over and over and over. It's like a washing machine, wash-rinse-spin. And if that one wears out, get a new one, but it's still the same routine, same old cycle."

"Divorce is the spin cycle, and I'm tired of spinning," I tell her.

"Maybe you should wash and rinse?" She screams.

"Maybe I should unplug?" I say. "I want to unplug and never see your face again. I'll never have to talk to you again. I'll rip the fucking cord out and be done. Fuck You!"

A rogue wave stands up in the darkness of the day as the rain blows sideways. I watch in a paralyzed state as it marches toward me. I look all around to see that I'm alone in this chaotic, turbulent body of water. The wave is going to crush me, and I really don't give a fuck. My wish has come true.

I scream out to the wave, "I'm good with dying. Please hold me on the bottom like a wrestler. I don't give a fuck!"

I don't try to paddle. I don't resist. I don't try to dive under. I'm letting this motherfucker have its way with me and drive me straight to hell. Actually, I'm pretty sure I've already been to hell.

"Take me someplace I've never been," I scream at it, "take me some place I've never been! Fuck you, life! Fuck you!"

The eighty-foot wave crashes over my head like a size 22 shoe stepping on an ant. I'm merely a spec of sand in the universe. The explosion of water engulfs my body as the sound is excruciating and the power is immeasurable. One hundred freight trains have collided, and I'm in the middle. The last thought in my head is, NOTHING.

I'm swirling and whirling in the current of life, like a feather being blasted by a jet engine. Every limb of my body feels as if it's going to be torn from my torso. I'm doing forced yoga poses that are horrific, but then doing yoga sucks anyway. I'm a rag doll being tortured by a sadistic three-year-old.

You'd think my brain would be screaming, SURVIVE. No way. Imagine being run over by a semi-truck. Your brain doesn't scream survive. It shuts down until the event is over, and that's exactly what I want to do. I want to become fish food. I want to go on a permanent shut down of life where I see no one again. I want to return to the place where it all began. I was born in water. Let me die in water. It's absolutely beautiful when you stop to think about the essence of being in water. It's calming and serene. It's truly a spiritual sensation that invokes joy, serenity, and calmness. I have crossed over at this point as my body is hurled through the deep darkness of the ocean in an uncontrollable manner. I've accepted my fate. I've accepted death. I've accepted all that is and will be.

The underwater tornado has subsided, and I'm suspended in the grasp of mother nature while floating on my back underwater, looking up to the rays of light shining down upon me. I don't know if I'm dead or alive.

A voice in my head asks, "Do you choose life or death?"

Before I can answer a single bright light hits me in the face and blinds me as it approaches my being. I feel like the decision has been made. I didn't get to answer the question. Is this the light of the universe coming to take me into another dimension? My mind thinks that the choice of death has been made for me. My brain is having second thoughts. I have chosen death. I shall make my last swim. I shall take my last breath. I shall never hear my kids laugh again. I shall feel no pain, ever again. I shall lose all worries. I shall live in eternal love. My thoughts feel so real and comforting except one.

"I shall never see my kids again."

My thought is interrupted as the blinding light and whirling electric motor stops in front of me, and the beautiful voice of Charlie calls out my name.

"West, my boy!"

I'm blown away by the fact that we can talk underwater. If we can communicate underwater, we can communicate anywhere, I think.

I'm not the little boy who got crunched by the wave. I'm the grown up who recognizes he has work to do.

Charlie's voice exudes excitement as he rides his ultra underwater cycle. The bike glides effortlessly through the ocean. Charlie smiles from ear to ear and fills my entire being with hope, trust, and courage.

"West, you did it! He shouts. "You survived the world's biggest wave. Look at you. You're a survivor. Get on! I have somewhere incredible to take you."

I pull myself onboard with little effort and gaze at the surface of the water as the rays of light spill across my face. I feel the power of the water and sun fill my body as Charlie turns to me and says, "You're not just a survivor. You're a warrior. Harness the warrior within your being and know there's a path that leads to love. I believe in you, West. It's your choice to choose the path of allowing or making it hard. West, remember this, Love is the most powerful emotion we can live from."

5

COURAGE

"Love calls for your courage to accept and forgive what is"

We motor along slowly under the surface of the ocean as the sun's rays penetrate the water, and golden light creates shafts of light. We wind our way through the kelp forest as if venturing deep into the woods of nature. The look is majestic because the kelp hangs from the surface to infinity. Charlie motors as if there is a path laid out before him. I know he's navigating by feel. This guy doesn't follow a path. He doesn't need to know where he is because he's going wherever he's pulled to go. We glide through the kelp forest and come to a stop. Everywhere I turn, all I can see is kelp and nothing else.

I feel the roar of anxiety creeping up my spine as silence engulfs my soul.

I tap Charlie on the shoulder and ask, "Do you have a GPS?"

He laughs with a mighty roar. "I have a PGS, personal guidance system. You are born with it, but most people turn it off around the age of thirteen."

I look at Charlie and realize what's coming next.

"Are you leaving me here to find my PGS?" I ask. "You're leaving me here in the middle of nothing?"

Charlie holds out his hand and pulls a strand of kelp.

"This is not nothing. This is life, food, oxygen, and it will cleanse your past, thus showing you your future."

"How am I supposed to get out of here?" I ask.

"If you had the answer, then you wouldn't be here," he tells me.

"West, you have so much to offer people, the world. It's time for you to swim." He pushes me off, and like that, He is gone. His under-water machine doesn't even leave a wake.

I sit there wondering about my PGS. Do I need batteries? I wonder. Then I think that's a stupid fucking question. The silence is deep. It penetrates my soul in a way I have never experienced. The kelp brushes against my skin and creates a soothing touch, but the feeling of loneliness is overwhelming. I sit there, wondering what the hell I am going to do or where I'm supposed to go. I spin in a 360-degree motion very slowly. My view is kelp. That's all I can see. Where am I supposed to go? I can't see anywhere. It's weird. I should feel trapped, but I don't. I've given up on figuring out how I'm breathing. I'm breathing under water. I think. How cool is that?

Still, I'm truly baffled as to why Charlie would leave me here. The kelp is so thick I can't swim. Am I supposed to swim? Is there something I'm supposed to get? Like an emotion, a feeling? I feel like I'm going through a car wash. The sensation of being trapped is entering my body. I'm really disliking the ability to escape the kelp. I've had enough. My anxiety level is slowly increasing. I would like a sign or maybe a mermaid to appear. I can't do anything. Do I fight it?

"Hello!" I scream out. "Is anybody else here?"

Even if someone else were around, I couldn't see them. Would I rather be stuck in kelp or the desert? If I were stuck in the desert, could I walk? Is it night or day? I don't like being hot, so I'll stay in the water.

This truly might be the worst joke someone could play on me. I'm almost ready to hit the panic button. The intensity of my energy is rising as my feeling of being trapped is escalating. The more my anxiety rises, the harder the kelp slaps my body. The kelp is alive.

Why am I in this? I love the ocean, but for god's sake, give me a better dream. Give me a dream with freedom. If I were a kelp farmer, I'd be rich. I'm not a farmer. I like to harvest waves. Kelp? What would I do with all this? I hear the voice of Bubba from Forest Gump. Kelp hats. Kelp belts. Kelp fries. Kelp smoothies. Kelp toilet paper. Kelp pizza. Kelp Jerky. BBQ kelp. Kelp shampoo. This is maddening.

"Shut up! Shut the fuck up! I get it, I got it. Kelp is good."

If I have another kid, I'll name it kelp. Kelp has no gender identity. It is neutral. What the hell? I'm putting way too many thoughts into it. This isn't a dream. It's a kelp mare! The thoughts of kelp have invaded every ounce of my brain. I couldn't go back in my thoughts if I wanted to. What if I focus on one leaf of the stalk and give it a name? I could give it a new identity. This is my game. I can make up my own rules. I'm going to call it My Game. I'm going to keep it simple, and the first rule will be, there are no rules. I frickin' love that. A game with no rules! Yeah. What if it's a game based on your thoughts? And all your thoughts would drive the game. I love the idea. This game is about using the kelp that annoys me. I'm going to hold a leaf and tell the first thought that comes into my head, and I have to tell my first thought in three seconds. I'm actually hearing myself talk. I sound different than I normally do. My voice tells me, "Go ahead, choose a leaf."

I extend my arm through the water and watch tiny bubbles chase along my hand as I reach out for a leaf. It waves in the depth of the water as if it's dancing. It truly seems to be saying, pick me. My eyes are fixated on the vast amount of textures and spine that runs the length of the leaf along with the multiple colors of green-ish/brown that's translucent. It's so soothing to the touch and yet so strong. I hold it and hear myself count back from three, three, two, one. One word spills off my tongue, Sadness. I feel like my conversation is with kelp and not myself. I recognize that the kelp is here to help. In a weird way, the kelp is an extension of me, sur-rounding me, protecting me, and I'm trusting it.

I hold the leaf as it speaks to me. "Why do you feel sadness?" The question seems so simple as if I could give a one-line answer and be done. The truth within me knows that's not true. Does this kelp bed hold deep wisdom? And here I am merely holding one leaf. I can't escape. I'm surrounded by the entire kelp bed with no place to go, no path. No way out.

The leaf speaks again.

"West, It's game on. What is the source of your sadness?"

I'm hesitant to talk about that. I feel as though I have one op-tion, and that's play the game. It's a moment in time when you re-alize there's no other way to process except doing what's presented to you. I hold the leaf as if it's the hand of my best friend, the friend that you can tell anything to. I reach deep into my soul to find my sadness. What is my sadness? I rub the leaf with my other hand and feel every bump and detail, but what I really feel is that it's a source for love, compassion, clarity, and understanding. I don't truly understand or comprehend what is happening, but I'm compelled to do it. My words can't describe the feeling. All I know is that I'm rubbing the leaf like it's a genie bottle. I'm not sure if I'm nervous. I'm not sure if I have anxiety. I'm not sure if I have fear. I'm not sure if it's grief. For each moment I hold the leaf, my trust rises. I'm starting to wonder if the leaf is holding me. Maybe this entire kelp forest is holding me in love. I want to feel it. I want to be here. And I know I should be.

In order to stay here, I have to answer the question. Why do I feel sadness? Tears roll from my cheeks and expand into bubbles as they float into the ocean. Within the bubble of the tear is a loving photo of my wife and me on our wedding day. She's holding a handful of flowers at my crotch. Our faces are filled with laughter and love. We're laughing with pure joy. The bubble spins slowly in the water, radiating and reflecting multiple colors. There's a sense of soothing when I gaze upon it. The colors of the bubble blend together, and the sadness of extinction overwhelms the bubble. I reach out with my hand to hold it one last time, gently, while the image slowly rotates around inside. The simplicity of the bubble disappearing into the kelp forest is magical. The magic is that the bubble is opening a path through the kelp.

There's a deep sadness in the pit of my stomach as the memory of my wedding day slips away. It's as if it never happened. The feeling of knowing each other is gone. The joy is gone. The laughter is gone. The love is gone. We became robots, getting through the day, which became years, and now here I am. I want to hold the tear one more time so I can feel what we once had. The sadness lives on as if I bought something, and the clerk gave me change. What I bought didn't last, and the coins represent the accumulation of dreams, hope, fears, trust, and sadness that's stored in a jar. Do the coins hold value, or are they just change? I don't know. I once heard someone say change is inevitable.

The sadness of my marriage navigates its way through the kelp forest. It's peaceful in a way although the tears keep rolling, and there's a tightness in my throat with my lips quivering. My body feels like one big brick. I see love in the bubble, and the sadness in my body is overwhelming.

Another tear forms in front of me. It has grown to a huge bubble filled with an image. The hospital room is packed with flowers and shafts of golden light pouring in. My wife holds a beautiful baby boy under her arm as they lie sleeping in the bed. The room holds peace and love while I stand over them in amazement, knowing I have a child. I never thought that would happen, but there I am, married with a fresh new soul who's come into the world to live. I stare into the bubble of love and see a man who's scared. His fear, my fear, is washed away by the power of love as he leans over the bed to kiss the baby boy on the head and gently hold his tiny fingers with his big hands.

I think to myself, "I shall walk with you forever. I will give you everything my dad couldn't show me. I will say I love you. I will hug you tightly. I will allow tears of joy, sadness, and love to flow down your face. I will always be here for you. I'm your dad. I will always be your dad."

I smile at my wife and lean over to kiss her forehead. She disappears from the bubble. A pillow lies on the bed where she once was. It's a black pillow with white letters. The letters spell out, DIVORCED.

I made a promise to this baby that I will give everything my dad couldn't. My dad was divorced, and now I am too. The sadness of failure engulfs my being. I've broken my promise. What is the value of my word? I want to be a success to this child. I want to be my best for him. I want to give love with no expectation. Who am I? If I'm no better than the man before me. The tear bubble floats through the kelp as the leaves gently caress it.

I'm sad because I failed at my marriage. I'm sad that I failed you, Zang. The tears appear to be light, airy, and bouncy. I know differently. I feel the heaviness, the weight of sadness. I see it. I feel it. I taste the salt as if the entire ocean is one big tear. The tears keep rolling down my cheeks as a blue tear suspends in front of my face with a shaft of golden light spilling over the top of it.

Within the tear bubble, I see my second child born. She is beautiful with her angelic skin and strawberry blond hair. She radiates love while lying in her mom's arms. They're being pushed through the hospital in a wheelchair. I'm walking in front of them while smiling from ear to ear. I'm so proud to have this beautiful being enter the world. My three-year-old son walks beside me, holding on to one of my fingers.

This little baby girl is our family angel, a blessing. She brings harmony and balance to our family. I love the feeling of being a dad. I'm proud. I cherish this moment, and when I think it can't get any better, my baby girl smiles. Our two-day old baby girl smiles at the world. My heart leaps out of my chest with so much joy, and I feel whole and complete.

We stop at our car. I gently lift my son into his car seat and turn and gingerly place my daughter in hers. I turn to help the kid's mom from the wheelchair. She's gone. The wheelchair is gone. There's a suspended black sheet of paper with big white letters that reads, DIVORCED. I stand there staring at it. I turn to the kids as the heavy weight of failure rests on my shoulders. The sadness feels unbearable as I watch the tear bubble flow through the kelp. I observe the kelp gently caress the bubble as it flows through. I feel the heaviness of my heart, and my soul is lost. With each tear that falls from my cheek, a bubble is formed. I feel compelled to follow the path that the bubble creates. It's a pulling of my soul to follow, and I don't realize until after it's happening. The tears are real, and they're heavy. I know I've never cried this much before. Being encapsulated by the ocean is comforting while I allow the flow of tears. I don't fight it. My emotions feel heavy as if an anchor is holding me down. Do I need to swim for air? I stay where I am because I'm supposed to. Another bubble forms in front of me. I gaze into it like it's a snow globe. I see my entire family enjoying a trip to the snow-covered mountains. We're all dressed in cold-weather gear, holding our snowboards. I can't see the smiles, but I can feel them. I can hear the laughter and joy. I can feel the love from all of us together as a family.

I'm mesmerized by the bubble. I stare at the scene taking place before me. I see all of us climbing onto an over-sized rocking chair that's sitting beneath the snow-covered trees. The kids climb onto the chair first and sit at the edge with their feet and legs hanging off the edge. I watch as Dawn's snowsuit turns white. Her entire outfit blends into the snow, and she disappears. And just like that, she's gone. The moment happens so fast I'm not given a chance to react. I climb onto the rocking chair with my kids and pull them in tightly. The three of us sit in the chair while massive snowflakes fall onto our heads. The moment is peaceful, serene, and quite lonely.

I watch as the tear of loneliness floats through the kelp. The leaves of the kelp caress the sides of the tear as it makes its way through the forest as if it knows where it's going.

Another bubble forms quickly in front of me. I see Dawn climb onto the oversized rocking chair. The snowflakes are huge as they float to the ground. Her red hair glistens in the white of the image. Her snowgear is white. Everything in the bubble is white except for her hair that's flowing from under her beanie. I can't see her eyes. They're hidden behind the goggles covering her soul. The snowflakes increase in size and fill the space as her hand slowly waves goodbye with her fur-covered mitten. The wave is slow and steady and timed with the fading light.

The bubble glides through the kelp forest. I watch for what feels like an eternity of time as the tear is gently caressed by the flowing kelp leaves. The leaves double in size as the tear fades into the darkness of the forest.

Another huge tear rumbles off my chin and morphs into a giant bubble. It's the same scene, only this time I'm sitting on the rocking chair by myself. The chair is so big that I feel like a little kid as I sit in the middle of the chair with the arm rests out of reach. I scooch to the right and place my elbow on the snow-covered armrest. The snowflakes fall in slow motion. The flakes are falling so slowly that I can maintain focus on one flake at a time as it floats from the sky into my hand. I do this repeatedly as if they're a therapeutic valve. It feels good to sit here with no distractions or interruptions. The chair feels quite homey, and the snow is providing a sense of warmth. I feel I should be cold, I'm not. I watch as the snow lands in the same place on my glove. I want to feel the snow, so I pull my hand from my glove. It looks huge. How could it have fit inside my glove? All my attention is focused on my hand. I can't believe how big it looks.

The moment is interrupted when a huge man walks up to the chair. He's too big for it. Geez, how could someone be that large? He's frickin' huge. His goggles cover his face, but as I observe his mannerisms, I realize it's my dad. The goggles he's wearing are enormous with a reflective lens covering half his face. I can watch a movie off those lenses. His big bald head glistens in the faint light as the snow falls. He doesn't speak, and his demeanor is scary. He has big, bold energy.

I'm so intimidated to look at him without seeing his eyes, so I try to look through the lens of his goggles, but all I can see is myself.

Why is he standing here? I'm not doing anything. I feel pretty good. I'm one with nature, feeling semi at bliss, and then this abominable snow dad disrupts my peace and sends my blood pressure skyrocketing. I scream at him.

"Why are you here?"

He doesn't answer, he doesn't move. I can't find the courage to look at him. I try. I dig deep within my soul and see I have no support. I want to stand up to him. I want to punch him in the face. I want to destroy this monster in front of me, to destroy this human who stole my soul, this motherfucker who robbed me of my childhood.

I scream at myself. You coward! I'm exactly who he said I would be. He defined me, and I accepted it.

My dad grows right before my eyes. His size dwarfs me and makes me feel so small in size, mind, and soul. I am nothing. My only defense is to retreat into the kelp, and that's exactly what I do. I'm not ready to stand up to the monster in my dreams, or is it a nightmare? It doesn't feel like a dream. The emotions are real. I feel his larger-than-life presence. He was always so much bigger than everyone else and never took shit off anyone. Was he a man? I don't know.

Here I am hiding in the kelp from a guy I call Dad. As a kid, I would hide under my bed and in the closet. The closet was safe. The closet was a space no one ever invaded. The closet was my sanctuary where my deepest thoughts, emotions, and dreams were housed.

The kelp reads my thoughts and forms a small square cocoon that resembles a box big enough for me to fit in. I sit here wondering if I will ever have the courage to get out of the box. I think about the little boy who stood up to his dad with a butcher knife. I wonder about the little boy who pulled a gun on his dad. I wonder about the little boy who endured trauma day in and day out from the emotional, volcanic eruptions of his father. Why, as a man, can't I find the courage to stand up to the one person who created the damage?

I'm suspended in a state of weightlessness and surrounded by walls of kelp. It truly feels like there's no way out, and truthfully, I don't care. It feels natural to go here. I've been here a million times in my mind. This is home. This is peaceful. It's my hide out, the ultimate safe place.

I realize safe is keeping me from growing on a spiritual level. Being safe is my prison. Being safe is a place to just exist. What do I want to do? I needed a safe place as a child. Now is my time to confront all my childhood trauma that haunts my adult life. I feel like a rock that can't be broken, and that's not a good thing. How many years would it take for my rock to become grains of sand on the beach? I'm not sure my lifetime will support that emotional breakdown of emotional hardness. If I'm going to have a breakdown of emotions, now is the time. How?

I can see the breakdown. I can see the tears. I can see the memories. I feel trapped in my kelp box. Everywhere I look, I see only kelp. My mind races with so many thoughts that feel like rocket fuel with nothing to propel. I want out, want to do something. I have to get out of the kelp.

"Why am I stuck here? Am I stuck?"

How do I get out? I realize I need to look up. There it is, right in front of me. I see a clear-cut path leading to the surface of the water. The sun's rays light my way as I swim to the surface. There is nothing holding me back. I swim effortlessly to the top and punch through, and in a split second, I go from hearing my own thoughts to hearing the outside world of my existence.

I can no longer hear my thoughts. All I can hear is the roar of white noise as a massive amount of white water comes screaming toward me. My mind says dive. I didn't want to and stay on the surface. The foam is thick and turbulent; it pushes me around like I'm nothing.

The roar of the water engulfs my senses. My eyes can't cut through the pea soup fog that encapsulates my vision. I can't see anything and can't feel the bottom.

The voice in my head keeps screaming, "Do something! What are you going to do?"

I want to take action, but my thoughts are frozen, non-existent. Is this where I die? Is this death? I guess it is. I guess today is a good day to die. I feel like a cat flailing around in a bathtub. Do I say anything before I die? There's no need to text or do Facebook live or create an Instagram story. I'm going to die a simple death. It's a death nobody has to clean up, a death in the water, the same place I came from. I'm returning to the womb of the universe. I can accept that. I can totally accept that. It's warm, cozy, and a little larger. It's a little loud though.

The roar of an engine echoes in the fog. Hope catapults from my thoughts. I'm going to be rescued. I'm saved. Today is not my day to die. The sound of the jetski draws near. My body fills with excitement in anticipation of my rescue. I'm saved!

I see Charlie riding on the ski. The fog lifts as he rides directly at me. The sun shines upon us as Charlie brings peace, calmness, and clarity. The ocean transforms into a tranquil deep blue with an ultra-smooth surface. The wake of the ski is the only ripple in the water. I wave too Charlie as he waves back.

"What are you doing?" He asks as he circles me.

"I'm waiting for my pizza to be delivered. I don't know how to answer your question."

"Although your decision to swim up seems perfectly logical, it's not," he says. "It's as if you soaped up in the shower and then stepped out to dry off before rinsing."

"Charlie, I've been underwater crying my eyes out," I tell him. "What more do you want from me?"

"I want you to finish cleansing yourself. I want you to wash the soap off. Crying is good. Crying releases all your pent-up emotions that have been stored in your cells for an enormous amount of time. West, it's time to have the courage to finish what's been started. Courage to rinse the soap. Courage to go under and let the kelp cleanse you. Courage to follow the path the kelp creates for you. You have to trust in the process. It's time to go back and finish your work."

"How long am I supposed to be underwater?" I ask.

"West, do you ask yourself how long you should take to rinse the soap from your body?" He says. "No. You do it until you're clean. When you find the courage to accept, forgive, and love yourself and others, you'll be clean. You'll feel whole. Life will become clear to you."

"What if I want to stay right where I am?" I ask.

"West, do you want to continue to live a life filled with sadness, anger, fear, and self-destruction? What if every day could be filled with love and courage?" He doesn't give me time to think, and he throws a tow line from the jet ski. "Grab the line, West. I'm towing you into the biggest wave of your life."

Charlie spins the ski around and tosses me the line. He pauses for a moment and then says, "West, when you catch the biggest wave of your life, how will it feel?"

"Euphoric," I scream out.

"Wouldn't you want to store that euphoric feeling in your body?" He asks, and when I nod, he says, "Then why are you hanging on to the bullshit of childhood?"

I hold the ski handle close to my chest as the roar of the jet ski comes to life. I'm holding the handle with an over/under grip. I lean back in the water and stretch my legs out in front of me with my knees pulled into my chest and my feet in the straps of the orange tow board. The nose of the board pokes its way to the surface as the power of the ski pulls me to an effortless glide. I'm not thinking about anything. I'm focused on making the drop and getting the wave of a lifetime. My heart pumps as I relax my forearms and watch Charlie steer the ski. His every move is so precise as he steers with confidence. He doesn't ask me if I'm ready. He observes my position in the water. He observes my head nod. And just like that, I skim out on the face of the wave, leaving the tow rope behind. It's as if Charlie and I have been tow partners for years. I don't question his ability and he doesn't question mine. I'm so focused I don't hear a sound. My momentum builds as I plane down the face of the giant moving mountain of water. The face of the wave is perfect and glassy. There's no wind. No chop. The conditions couldn't be more epic. I'm gliding at the perfect speed with very little effort. It's almost too easy. The golden sun cascades light upon me as I ease my way down the face of the wave in slow motion. This is by far the best wave I have ever ridden. I couldn't dream of a better one. This moment is pure ecstasy, pure ecstasy. I feel at one during this seven second ride on the amazing natural beauty of Mother Nature. My adrenaline is pumping as I release the rush of my ride through a giant exhale and fly off the lip, launching myself into the air. I hear the monstrous swoosh as this beauty closes out, and a wall of white water explodes into the air. This mountainous beauty releases all her energy with a mighty roar and spit.

I fly so high and for so long with my leash tugging on my ankle as it stretches from my board. The smile I feel spreading across my face says it all. I am consumed by the rush of adrenaline. I want more. I need to have this sensation for the rest of my life. I'm on top of the world while floating in the abyss of nothingness.

I tug on my leash and pull my board to me, and all in the same motion, I am on my board, paddling toward Charlie as he approaches on the ski. He spins the sled toward me, and I pull myself on effortlessly. I am elated, blown away by the thrill of accomplishment.

I thrust my hands into the air and scream, "I did it."

Charlie high fives me and guns the throttle to get us to safety. My entire body vibrates as we race across the water. I've surfed the biggest wave of my life and I am stoked!

The moment is short lived as Charlie pulls a bright red 10' 6' gun from nowhere. The surfboard look amazing. It is amazing.

"You can do it," he says. "I want you to paddle into the bomb of your life."

I want to celebrate my tow-in wave. Why can't we just celebrate my last one? The pit of my stomach churns as my nuts retreat to my gut. I look at Charlie like a deer in the headlights.

"It's fucking huge, not just big. It's fucking huge."

Charlie sits there like it's no big deal. He has all the confidence in the world. He doesn't flinch, doesn't hesitate. His emotions and demeanor are solid, He's a source of energy and inspiration. In my head, I'm thinking, I'm the one who has to paddle out. It seems really easy to sit in the channel and exemplify confidence and courage. Let's see him go sit on the peak and watch mountains of water race toward him.

I can only equate it to trying to swim up Niagara Falls. Good luck. It's completely impossible. Charlie doesn't give me a choice. He's serious.

"What if I don't do it?" I ask.

"You tell me," he says. "What would that feel like?"

I think long and hard, I truly want to understand my feelings and emotions. I want to understand Charlie's intentions.

"What can I gain and what can I lose?" I ask him.

"What could you lose?" He repeats.

"Death" I say. "I could die."

"You're dead if you don't do it," he tells me. "You need courage to operate in love. Love your fear. Love your disappointment. Love who you are."

"How did I go from feeling pure stoke too feeling lost?" I ask him.

"Because I put you in an uncomfortable position, and in your mind, you can't see yourself doing it," he says. "So, you're going to quit before you ever start. You need to know that there's a KNOW-ING within the universe that is bigger than all of us, and you have to trust it. I'm your guide, trust me. I know you can do it. You've surfed this wave a million times in your head. Repeat these words, paddle, commit, make the drop. You've made that drop a million times. What's one more? There's not much difference between a million and a million and one. You got this."

The calmness in his voice runs down my spine and tethers all the courage bubbling from my cells. He's right. I have made this drop a million times. I never thought about how. I just did it. I would hide in my closet as a kid and mind surf wave after wave, ride my motorcycle, fly like a bird. I used my mind to escape and to survive. I survived every time. I made the drop every time. I never wiped out. I never crashed. I was the hero of my journey.

Charlie slows the ski down as I dive off the back and pop up to the surface of the water. I looked at Charlie sitting on the ski and glowing a bright gold. His glow is magical. It brings me comfort and means everything to me. He looks at me and pierces my soul with love I can feel and see. I knew that with this much love I could do it.

"West, he says, "I love you."

"I know, Charlie. I know."

Just then, a big black cloud rolls in and the sun disappears. The wind sweeps through as I sit on my board and wrap my leash around my ankle.

Then I drop my leg into the water, lay my chest on my board, let my arms pull me across the water, and watch the big, black clouds roll across the sky.

"West," Charlie shouts. "The sun always shines, even when you can't see it."

I'm ready. I don't think about the dark clouds or the sun. I paddle with strength, feeling stronger than I ever have. I repeat Charlie's words in my head—paddle, commit, make the drop. Paddle, commit, make the drop.

I take small breaths in and out as I tell myself I truly love this moment. I love the clouds. I love the ocean. I love my board. I take my last stroke to put myself in the perfect spot. Then, I push myself up, sit on my board and wait for a set to come. I don't think about anything else. My focus is to catch a wave. I repeat to myself, commit, make the drop. Commit, make the drop. Commit, make the drop. Commit, make the drop. I keep the mantra going. The repetition of repeating those words keeps me calm and focused. The mantra tells my brain and body that I am ready. It delivers a message to every cell in my body that I am committed, and nothing can stop me. I repeat the words so many times that I barely realize my lips are moving. The mantra puts me in a hypnotic state of awareness and brings courage to my entire being. I am courageous. I am a gladiator. I am going to commit and make the drop.

I felt my self rise as three massive mountains of water roll under me. I tune out the black sky and howling winds. My million and one ride is coming. I know it. I can feel it. I keep repeating my mantra, commit, make the drop. And without realizing, I have turned and am paddling for the bomb of the day, making a commitment to catch this wave.

My body knows what to do. My feet hit the deck of the board like a cat, my balance solid and perfect. I'm free-falling from the top of the wave with the board perfectly placed under my feet. The sensation seems to last for minutes. My board feels amazing as I land with ease at the trough of the wave. I jam my bottom turn right into the pocket as this behemoth wave pitches its mighty lip over my body. This is by far the biggest, most cavernous barrel I have ever ridden. Sheer elation engulfs my body as I watch in slow motion. I can see every detail of the water rushing over my head. I can see the ribs of the wave as if it were the inside of a Wooly Mammoth. I'm inside the belly of the beast and loving every minute, every second, actually. Time doesn't matter. Only the moment does. I stay in the moment as a massive swoosh of wind comes from behind me and spits me out of the mouth of the beast. I know I'm smiling. I must be. My heart is pounding, excitement spews from my body. My heart pumps with so much adrenaline that it drowns out the sound of all the crashing waves and the sound of Charlie's ski.

I celebrate alone. If you do something amazing and all by yourself with no one around to see it and share the experience, did it really happen? How do I know it happened? I did it. I know I did it. But there is no one there to celebrate my experience. I sit there feeling alone. I wanted to feel joy, exuberance, and ecstasy. As hard as I try, the emotions won't come through. This can't be for nothing. I'm supposed to feel emotions. The weather around me is complete and utter chaos. Big black clouds roll overhead as the wind blows in excess of 35 knots. The sea is dark and uninviting with waves crashing into each other. The disorganization is overwhelming. I feel like I'm the one creating all this disorganization around me. I'm creating the mess. Did I create this storm? I want to run, to hide. I'm sitting in the middle of the ocean with nowhere to go. I'm not lost. I'm stuck. I know it's mental, but it's all around my physical world. I'm feeling so stuck and not quite sure what to do. What the hell do I do? I can't sit here forever. I feel the emotional wave of defeat pouring over me. My head slumps over as my chin hits my sternum. How do I move forward? I brush my hair out of the way as I sit staring down at my board. I see a wooden door on my board. The door appears to be huge and old. It doesn't look inviting but what other options do I have? I use all my energy to open this massive door. I pull on the handle with all my might. The door gradually opens with a groan, and there stands Charlie. He holds his hand out for me to join him.

"Come in," he says.

I stare at the door and wonder if I can fit though it.

"If you believe you can, then you can," he tells me.

I don't know what to believe. How the hell am I supposed to fit though the door? My mantra comes to mind, and the words fill my thoughts, Commit and make the drop. Commit and make the drop. Commit and make the drop. And just like that, I drop right through the door and am on the other side. My entire being feels so at ease, so calm.

Then, Charlie erupts with a pure stoke of animation. "How was that wave? That drop was insane! I'm so proud of you, West! I've never seen someone get so deep into the barrel. I knew you were coming out! Holy crap, you were so deep! You did it! You made a commitment and stayed out of your head. You put yourself in the unthinkable position and made it. That took fucking courage! All that courage resides in your soul and deep in your cells. Do you feel it? You can tap that courage anytime life gets challenging. It's a switch. West. Turn it on when you need it."

"Yeah! I feel it. I want to always feel it. I want to know it's there for me when I need it."

Charlie holds his hands out wide and glows with love

for me.

"West, I'm offering you the opportunity to face the loneliness you felt today. Make a commitment to yourself, to your soul, to your well-being, to your children. In this moment, you will commit to accepting what comes up. You will accept whatever comes up while you swim through the kelp forest. You will accept your sadness, you will accept your fears, accept your anger, you will accept your abuse and self-destruction. Because today you commit to having all the courage in the universe flowing through you. You have it. You didn't need to ride the biggest wave in the world to find courage. It wasn't in the wave. It was within you. The smallest events in life oftentimes require the most courage. Are you ready? Are you ready for an amazing journey though the kelp?"

I stare at the kelp that seems to go on forever with no end in sight.

"I don't know where to begin," I tell Charlie. "It's overwhelming. It's daunting."

"Yes, it's all of that, but just reach out and touch it."

I extend my hand slowly into the kelp and watch my fingers spread out and grasp the kelp leaf.

"West, did you tell your hand to open up?" He asks. "No. You didn't. Allow your body to flow through the kelp. It knows what to do. Don't think about it. Just commit and swim."

I find myself gliding effortlessly though the dense leaves and stocks of the kelp. Rays of sunlight penetrate the surface of the water and guide my way as the leaves gently brush against my skin and create a cleansing effect. The touch is totally cleansing my entire body and soul, and I want to stay in this calmness forever. How long could I actually stay here? Is this how my life will be forever from this day forward? My feeling of nothingness slowly turns to boredom. Am I really bored, I think? I'm able to breathe underwater. How can that be boring? How many people can breathe underwater? It doesn't matter. I am bored.

I close my eyes and glare at the reflections of light dancing inside my eyelids. I don't try to do anything. I let myself be. My intention is to be silent, not me, but my thoughts and emotions. My intention is to commit to nothing. That doesn't make sense to me though. Commit to nothing, I think. My whole life everyone has said you have to commit to something. Make a commitment to be a good person. You have to make a commitment to a girl, make a commitment to your job. How could I make a commitment to nothing? What is nothing, no thing? What's the difference between something and nothing?

All my physical strength seems to dissipate. I don't feel weak. I feel a sense of freedom. I stare at the seaweed in awe as it dances. I stare in awe as I wave. I stare as the currents around me push and pull on my body. I feel like a car going through the carwash. The currents propel me through this healing kelp that is cleansing my soul and emotions that I've been holding for a lifetime. I'm where I should be. I allow the flow to move me. I don't try to control it. I'm home in the water and home in my mind. The miracle of life is happening to me, and I am simply in the vortex of my universal essence.

The seaweed makes a path that I flow down with an effortless glide. I extend my arms out as I move through the kelp and gently touch the seaweed as I pass.

I look ahead to see a fork in my path, and my mind immediately goes into which way, left or right? The current begins to move at a faster pace, and my mind begins to race. Left or Right? Left or Right? Left or Right? Shit! Which way? Shit! Shit! Shit!

Charlie's voice interrupts my chaotic thoughts. "Commit to nothing." His voice is soft and soothing. He gives me comfort as I commit to nothing. I repeat the words after him: Commit to nothing. Commit to nothing. And in an instant, the flow slows down. The chaotic thoughts in my head dissipate. I allow the flow to take me to the right. I don't know why. I just do, and I'm ok with it. I go to the right, and my mind says, how easy was that? That was nothing.

BAM! My adrenaline spikes as the bottom drops out. My heart thumps, and my anxiety spikes while free falling with no idea how or where I am going to land.

6

FORGIVENESS

"Forgive the past so your love is everlast"

The fall has the exhilaration of riding the tallest roller coaster and making the descent from the front seat with my hands held high. The thrill doesn't last as I drop right into my childhood closet. My heart is racing and my adrenaline is pumping, but it isn't from the fall.

I've gone from the peaceful easy feeling of the kelp, to the confines of my childhood closet. I sit in the closet with my heart pounding and my breath pulsating. I'm terrified of the raging energy that exudes from my dad's billowing voice. I can hear him raging as he searches the house for me. I try hard to calm myself so he doesn't hear my breathing. I can't let him hear me.

He shouts, and I hear him punch the wall.

"Where are you, you little faggot?"

"Stop calling him names," my mom screams. "He's just a little boy."

I peer through a small hole in the door and watch as he shoves her to the ground. Why does he always come after me and my mom? What did I do?

The room goes silent, and I hear only my breath and my heart pumping in my chest. I take shallow deep breaths to calm myself. Finally, I feel myself breathing easier and with less effort, but I still feel my beating heart in my ears. The brief moment of silence feels good. Did he die of a heart attack? God, I hope so.

The closet door flies open. I gasp for air with the feeling of being trapped. I have nowhere to run or hide. He's found me. He grabs my arm with his huge bear claw and drags me from the closet.

I release my small, blue security blanket and reach for anything to grab as he drags me from the closet and across the floor. I'm scrambling to get to my feet. I'm almost there when he slams me against the wall. I bounce off of it and hit the ground, landing with my face pressed to the carpet and face to face with a red high-heel shoe. I've been playing dress up and wore my mom's shoes that day. My dad can't handle the thought of his son wearing women's high heel shoes. He freaked out and went ballistic on me, acting like this was a disgrace to his manhood. Now, he shouts with a vengeance as my mom tries to help.

I look up to see him take an open fist swipe at her, knocking her to the ground. The rage he harbors, spews from his soul at an uncontrollable level. He smashes my face to the carpet and makes me look at my mom's red shoes.

"What the fuck are you doing wearing your mom's heels? These are for girls! You have a cock! You're a man! Do you got a pussy in your pants? Jesus Christ, are you a little fag? Is that what you are? A little gay boy?"

I really don't understand what he's talking about. My mom inches her way close to me and mutters in a faint voice to my dad, "He's just a little boy."

He can't accept her words and stomps on her leg before she can move any closer to me.

"I got a queer little faggot bitch for a son." He looks up to the ceiling, "God! God! I'm fucking talking to you, you fucking asshole. What kind of God sends a little queer for a son?" He looks me dead in the eyes. "I catch you wearing heels again, I'll cut your fucking little pecker off."

I am mortified, and I don't know what to think except that this motherfucker has some serious problems. He storms out of the room with anger spewing from his fist as he puts another hole in my bedroom door, that's starting to look like a block of Swiss cheese. My mom lies there, battered and beaten, and in no shape to comfort me.

I hear a psst and turn to see me as an adult. A sense of relief overtakes my body as I run into the arms of my adult self. The adult hugs me with love and security; his hug is full of comfort and warmth.

"I love you," he says. "This is not your fault. You are an amazing kid who has so much to offer the world."

I can hug my inner child and give him strength and love for a moment, but no matter how many times I do this, it never seems to last. I can't accept the responsibility for forgiving my dad. I don't want to forgive him. I want to kill him.

I'm standing in the middle of a dark, tree-lined street with rows of houses on either side. I'm not sure which way to walk. I stare at the trees for answers and realize I haven't asked a question. I'm confused about what I should ask. What is my question? I'm not sure what to think. A single headlight approaches, and the familiar sound of Charlie's motorcycle roars to life. I feel comfort in knowing he's coming toward me. I feel grounded in knowing he will help me. I feel the loving power of his presence. I'm really trying to understand how much this guy means to me and my happiness.

The bike sputters to a stop. Charlie lifts his goggles and greets me with a smile.

"You're hanging out here in the street, doing nothing?" He asks.

I look around and say, "Yep, I guess so."

"Perfect," he says. The conversation feels awkward, as if we we are forcing words when words don't need to be spoken.

"Do you want to do something?" He asks.

"Sure," I say.

Charlie gestures for me to climb into the side car. I sling my right foot in and sit back in the seat. Then I pull my goggles over my eyes, and we speed off into the night with a trillion stars twinkling in the night. The stars feel so close that I reach out like a child, and think I can grab one.

Touch it, my mind says. As I focus all my thought on one star, it becomes so bright and grows in size, but as I try to grab it, I realize my arm isn't long enough. My mind tells me I can do it, so I keep trying for what feels like an eternity. Still, I keep trying as we ride through the night with the wind blowing across my face.

"Where are we going?" I finally ask him.

"Wherever the night sky takes us."

I'm not sure what he means, nor do I really care. I enjoy the calm of the night with the wind in my face and the stars encompassing our journey. The sense of freedom fills my body, and I ask myself, "Is this sustainable?"

The moment feels like it is going to be short-lived, I want to stay in it forever, to keep riding with Charlie. As soon as my thoughts turn elsewhere, that's what happens. I thought the ride would come to an end and it has. The motorcycle stops, and the air turns to a bitter cold.

I stand on the side of the road next to Charlie's motorcycle. The air seems to be getting colder, and the beautiful twinkle of the night sky begins to fade as the snowflakes grow in size. The only light I can see is a dull, blue one at the top of the mountain. Its light dims in and out as the snow fall increases. It seems so far away. It seemed so far away that I would have never thought about walking to it. I wondered why we've stopped. What am I supposed to do? Why are we here? Why am I here? The dim blue light has definitely caught my attention, maybe because it's the only thing to look at.

"Charlie, why am I here?" I ask.

"To accept and forgive," he tells me. "You're going to walk to the light on the mountain."

I point to the one and only light in the distance. "That one?"

"Yes, that one," he says. "It's the light of forgiveness, and in order to forgive, you have to accept. Do you accept where you are at this moment?"

"Do I have a choice?" I ask.

"Oh West, you always have a choice. It's the outcome you might not enjoy."

I rub the beautiful machine beside me. "Any chance I could get a ride?"

Charlie, with his infinite wisdom, answers, "Didn't you get a ride to here?"

"Yeah, but you're dropping me in the middle of nowhere."

"West," he says. "Nowhere is always somewhere."

The light seems so far out of reach. How can I ever make that kind of distance especially in the snow and cold? This moment seems like a cruel joke.

"How am I supposed to get through the snow?" I ask him. "Any chance I can get a cool motorcycle with a track for a rear wheel? That would be really cool."

"Two feet" He answers. "You have two feet, and if you want, I can give you snow shoes."

It's going to be freezing cold trudging through four feet of snow with snowshoes. Who the hell wants to do that? Snowshoes suck. I want a blazing hot fireplace, and a warm bed, my faithful Golden Retriever sitting on my feet while I drink a hot cup of coffee.

Charlie hears all my thoughts.

"You sure have a long list of things you think you need to make the journey," he says, "all of which will get you nowhere. Why don't you take a minute and look at yourself and see what you have?"

In my mind, I have nothing. What the hell is Charlie talking about? I feel naked in the wilderness without the comforts of home or what I thought was home. I don't have a tent, sleeping bag, heater, compass, goggles.

"West," he says. "You're telling me everything you don't have. I want you to look at what you do have."

I feel my chest and realize that I have a coat on.

"I have a coat."

"That's not just a coat," he says. "Feel it, look at it. It's everything you need to keep you warm. Within the coat, is everything you need to keep you moving toward the light. If you look outside the coat, you're not going to find what you need. Look at where you're standing. This is paradise. You are surrounded by a beautiful night sky with mountain ranges hugging you from the distance. The falling snow is a reminder that we are all one and unique in our own way."

Charlie tosses my snowshoes to the ground. I step with my left foot first and buckle in. The snowshoes make me feel ready. Then, there's a shift within my thoughts that make me feel more than ready.

My decision to accept my journey has a comforting feeling. I feel at peace with my decision even though I'm not sure if it was my decision or Charlie's decision.

I look at Charlie and say, "I'm ready. I accept this journey."

"I have one last thing for you, West." He hands me a bright orange pair of goggles with mirrored lenses. "Your perpetual journey of life will be seen through these goggles. Keep them on until you get to the beacon. Once you're at the light, you may remove them. Do not remove them until you get there."

I have to ask, "And if I don't keep them on?"

Charlie laughs, "You'll die in a fiery plane crash." He keeps laughing and finally says, "Nothing will happen. Absolutely nothing. No thing."

I'm not quite sure how to interpret his answer. What does he mean by nothing? What is nothing? The word sounds so weird. It echoes in my mind, no thing, no thing, no thing. I don't have the capacity to figure this out, and I guess I really don't care. I'm being sent out in the snow by Charlie and made to feel like it was my idea. I've never worn snowshoes before and yep, they're awkward.

I feel like James Bond could appreciate my coat. It seems to hold all the goods for my journey, and my bitchin' orange goggles will show me the way, or I can wear them while doing road construction. The ultimate would be to drop me at the beacon with my snowboard and I can blast my way down through some deep pow. Where's Charlie's sense of fun?

"West, I hear you," he says. "How do you know I didn't bring the snowboard? I have everything I need in life, and so do you."

And in an instant, I'm alone, standing under the night sky. The clouds hang low as the snow continues to fall. I take one last gaze at the beacon, and Charlie's words echo in my mind. "The beacon of forgiveness." The blue light has an intoxicating effect with it's magical glow. I'm captured by the light and feel the pull of its power. I inhale deeply and slowly release my breath as I pull the goggles over my eyes.

In that instant my world changes, and I'm put into a place and circumstance I don't want, an event I've relived a thousand times, make that one thousand and one.

I desperately try to lift the goggles from my face, but it's as if they're welded to me. I use all my focus to lock my attention on the beacon light and walk toward it. The feeling of sadness overwhelms me. The feeling is cold as I experience the embrace of Dawn's last hug. The hug where she asks for a divorce. The hug of goodbye. I lock my vision on the beacon and let the light give me hope. I can't escape the emotions I'm feeling or the vision I'm seeing from inside my goggles. I can see the hug, and the goggles allow me to focus on the beacon.

The beacon is my compass. In that moment, I know I must put my awareness on the hug and keep the beacon in my sightline. My focus is purely emotional. Dawn stands there, physically holding me with her emotions, pushing me away. How is this even possible? I'm getting a physical hug, and yet her emotions are shoving me far far away. I desperately try to understand, but the moment doesn't feel comprehensible. How do you comprehend rejection? How do you understand throwing twenty years of marriage in the garbage? How do you comprehend not kissing your kids before bed every night? How do you comprehend what love is? How do you comprehend your life? How do you comprehend your broken soul? How do you comprehend moving forward and living?

All I can do in this moment is walk. I have no choice. I walk and I walk and walk. I set my sight on the beacon and put one foot in front of the other because that's all my subconscious thought will allow. The sound of the shoe is soft and quiet as it moves through the snow, like a soft blanket. My body movement feels robotic and heavy. I keep repeating to myself, "one step at a time."

The time on a clock doesn't matter, it was irrelevant. Charlie didn't set a time to meet. My focus is not about time or meeting. My focus is all about Dawn's hug. I fixate on her cold embrace. I fixate on her words, "I want a divorce." They keep repeating in my head. "It's over West, I want a divorce." Her voice is direct and stern, A voice I have never heard and one I'll never forget.

I wonder about the twenty years of marriage we invested in

ourselves and our children. Why would we throw them away? Is she going to tell me why? Why seems like a really big word right now. Why also seems like it has no meaning or that it really doesn't matter. Why becomes irrelevant. I don't want why. I want how. How can we fix it? How do we keep our marriage together? There was no middle ground. And if there is, I don't see and can't feel it. All I feel is the ice-cold hug of goodbye. It's not really a hug though. It's more like a plunge in glacier water, the kind of plunge that numbs and wakes you all in one second.

That's what happened with Dawn and me. I stood in her embrace desperately wanting to feel. All I felt was numb. I wanted to love, and all I felt was numb. I wanted answers. All I got was numbness. The five-second, ice-cold hug robbed my soul of joy, passion, and purpose. Where do I go? What do I do? I had no energy to react. I had nothing in my tank of wellness. I was frozen in time and needed help. I silently whispered for a guide. I silently whispered for someone to help. My whisper was soft and almost silent because I had no voice, I had no strength. I had nothing to give myself except my faint quest for help.

The snow comes down in massive amounts with flakes the size of my fists. The wind blows from behind as if someone is pushing on my back. I have no choice but to walk in the direction the wind is blowing.

"West."

The sound of Charlie's voice brings strength to my soul, and the sight of him coming toward me with a snowboard attached to his feet and the wind propelling his bright fluorescent orange kite, gives me hope. He glides effortlessly toward me, making it look so easy as if he is cruising with not a care in the world. He is one with the board, kite, wind, and snow. He decelerates the kite and stops next to me.

"West," he says. "Turn toward the wind, accept what comes up, and forgive. It's time to forgive, no matter what." Before I can react or even think about his words, he tosses me another pair of goggles. "Put these on."

These googles are larger with a dark mirrored tint lens. I look at myself in them and see snow hanging from my red cheeks. I look as though I've been walking in the snow for years. My eyes look hollow, and I can't see a soul. There's zero life exuding from my being. How is putting on another pair of goggles going to help me? I think it's stupid, in my head, but my body wants a new set of goggles.

Without realizing, I put the new goggles on, right over the top of the old ones. There I stand with two sets of goggles on. A big puff of wind blows in my face and fills my ears with a deafening sound. Then silence engulfs me as I stare at the view from within my new set of goggles.

It is thanksgiving again, and I'm in 5th grade—again. Why? I truly don't want to relive this memory. I attempt to remove the goggles with no luck. They won't come off, and I have to watch the scene unfold once again.

This time is different. The table is set in the middle of the field with heavy snow falling. I can see myself as a little boy, sitting at the table with my head down. I feel alone. I feel ashamed. I feel scared. I don't want to sit at the table. I wanted to be anywhere except there with father and my anxiety at an all-time high in anticipation of what might set the beast off. The snow continues to dump, but it only falls on me.

I stick my tongue out to catch a flake just as my dad steps into the scene, and smacks me in the head, and says, "Have some manners."

His wedding ring feels like a hammer hitting my head. The sound echoes in my skull. I don't say a word in fear that an eruption of anger will follow. But when he wasn't looking, I flip my middle finger at him and feel good to quietly give a "fuck you" to him. Then, I quickly slide my middle finger across my eye as if I have an itch.

The glow of two white candles gives, the illusion of peace, and a perfectly cooked, golden brown turkey sits in the middle of the table. I'm fixated on the steam rising from it, and I realize I'm the only one noticing falling snow.

It's snowing in our house, I think, and no one has said a word. My dad makes it seem normal. Do I say something? Is anybody going to say something? Is anybody going to notice?

I avoid eye contact with my dad as I gaze at how nice the table looks. I stare at the stuffing sitting next to the turkey. I love stuffing and pretend to stare at the food although I'm really looking at my dad. He has no clue that I'm watching him. He sits there, stone faced, no expression, like a rock sitting in a chair accumulating snow. And out of nowhere the candles lose their flames. The smoke spirals to the ceiling or what appears to be a ceiling. The snow intensifies as the smoke spirals upward.

My mom is in the kitchen, hustling to finish the gravy, which she pours into a blue bowl. She carries it to the table as the rock comes to life.

My dad's reaction appears to be in slow motion as his fist comes across the table and hits me right in the face. At the moment his fist strikes my cheek, he shouts. "What the fuck." Your mom has been cooking all day, she sets this beautiful table, and you blow out the fucking candles. What a little twat you are."

I sit there in disbelief, but not really. The snow intensifies as the snowflakes increase in size. It's really coming down, and nobody says a word. Not one word. Are these guys insane? That's all I can think. My mom and dad are both insane. Nobody has noticed the frickin' snowstorm.

My mom places the blue bowl of gravy on the table and tries to relight the candles. She clicks and clicks and clicks the lighter and shakes it vigorously, like that's really going to help. She tries one more time to light the candles, but It's a no go.

My dad snatches the lighter from her hand, saying "Give me the goddamn thing." He makes several attempts to light the candles with no success.

I laugh. I don't know why. I just have to. It's snowing on our table, the candles won't light, and I'm the only one to notice the snowstorm. How can I not laugh?

My laughter is gasoline on my dad's fire of rage. He flips his lid and wipes the entire table clean. Another turkey dinner swept onto the floor by this human I call father. I try to grab the stuffing before it goes flying across the room, but I fail. My dad's face is beet-red as anger spews from his eyes. He sounds and looks like a demented teenager.

"Why are you laughing?" He demands.

The snow is falling heavier and heavier. It has covered the table and the mess on the floor. It has covered everything.

I look at my dad and stare deeply into his soul. For the first time in my life, I'm not scared, not ashamed, and not embarrassed. I realize his rage was his. It has nothing to do with me, and I'm truly okay with this situation. I accepted it.

I open my mouth and slowly stick out my tongue, allowing the snow to fall on it. My dad sits there watching, and in that moment, I realize I didn't do anything wrong. All this rage and anger was his. I am a kid, sitting at the table, trying to cope with adults who don't know how to cope with life. All I want is to catch a snowflake. All I want is a peaceful dinner.

I catch one last snowflake with my tongue and can't believe the words that come from my mouth.

"I forgive you," I tell my dad.

He doesn't have a response, and I don't need one. He looks like a grizzly bear who doesn't know if he should attack or run. I stare at him, wondering if he feels anything and if he can feel any emotion other than anger. Where does all his anger come from? I have questions, but I know he's not capable of answering them because he's not ready. He doesn't want to know himself, and he's stuck in thinking that he should be someone who he thought he was, His version of a man.

He's a sad, pathetic human trapped in the existence of his ego, He's just a boy who aged, and I recognize that the only way I can escape his anger, rage, and judgement is to forgive him. I know this will bring sunshine to my life. And so I say again, "I forgive you, Dad. I forgive you."

The snow stops instantly as the sun casts its rays upon me. I feel free. I feel liberated. The sky is crisp and blue, and the warmth feels like a great cup of hot coffee after a cold morning surf. I watch the steam from my breath as the sun's rays reflectivity bounce off the pure white snow. My goggles don't seem to cut the brightness, and I become snow-blind in a field of white with no visual on the beacon. I have no clue which way to walk and can't see my tracks. There is nothing in front of me and nothing behind me. Amazingly, I don't feel lost.

I have no idea what I'm supposed to do or where to go. The crisp blue sky quickly becomes covered in fast-moving billowy clouds. The clouds capture my attention with their excessive movement. They look very unnatural.

The quiet swoosh sound of a snowboarder captures my attention. He's gliding effortlessly across a field. A flat field. He isn't going down a mountain. He's just gliding across that field with deep powder snow and making huge carves that throw massive walls of spray. It is truly art in motion. The carves are slow and meticulous, and I'm mesmerized.

I love watching the display of talent and grace and soon realize it is Charlie riding his board with such magic. I spin in a circle as he carves a 360 around me, at one with the board and snow. He throws the board sideways and stops in front of me as a wall of snow flies over my head. Damn, he's good.

"West my boy, where are you going?" He asks.

"I'm not sure," I say. "I can't see the beacon. I can't see my tracks."

Charlie holds out another set of goggles.

"West, you can't look at your tracks. You gotta go deep, my son, you gotta go deep."

He handed me the goggles. "Put these on, and they will help guide you to the beacon."

I stared at his snowboard, hoping he'll grant my wish.

"Is there a chance I can ride your snowboard? I could definitely get to the beacon fast on your board, Charlie."

His laugh is filled with love and encouragement laced with comfort.

"West, this board is made for me and me only. It would do you no good, but get to the beacon and I'll have your board waiting for you, and it will be just as magical."

"Is there any chance you could make it black and orange?" I ask.

"West, you make it to the beacon, and I'll have a magic black and orange board for you."

I don't waste another minute. Charlie says two words as I pull the new pair of goggles on.

"Accept and forgive. Those are the two words that will get you to the beacon. I believe in you, West."

Then, I watch in amazement as he carves his way across the field, throwing walls of snow with each carve. God, I want to ride his board. He leaves walls of snow floating in the air with each carve, and the crystals form end-to-end rainbows across the field. What a bitchin' site. I can see myself riding it as Charlie disappears into the trees.

Now, I'm alone with a pair of goggles that will show me the way to the beacon. All I wanted is that new magic board. Show me the way, goggles. I pull them over my existing goggles. It feels a little silly but oh so right. I take a long, deep breath and face the haunting memories hidden within the goggles.

My eyes adjust to the darkness, and with a flick of a switch, I'm standing in the kitchen with my mom. I'm seven years old, and it's Christmastime.

My mom and I are baking Christmas cookies. I've analyzed this moment a thousand times but never understood it. I was a mere seven years old and had lived through more rage and highly charged emotional outbursts, and I'd witnessed my mom take severe ass kickings by my dad. There were times I thought my arms were broken from the twists, shoves, and beat downs by him.

But today it is me and my mom baking cookies. She lets me wear an apron so I could feel like a real baker. I help her roll out the dough. She sets me up with my own area on the counter. I'm proud that I can roll out the dough so well, and the moment is filled with joy and peace. I love the thought of making cookies for my cousins, aunts, and uncles. I press cookie cutters into the dough and make circles, Christmas trees, and gingerbread men. The freshly baked cookies are cooling on the kitchen table. I've brought them to life with red and green sprinkles, and I'm proud.

WHAM! The sound of the front door slams shut.

My mother scurries over to remove my apron. I don't want to take it off, proud that I'm a baker. The energy in the kitchen turns tense and eerily quiet. My mom turns off her radio. We can hear the thunderous footsteps thud across the living room and into the kitchen.

My dad stands in the doorway of the kitchen, glaring at all the cookies. He looks huge, like a gorilla or maybe a bear. He stares at the cookies for so long his face distorts with discomfort. I've seen his look a million times, and it never has a happy ending. He's a walking time bomb that has no fuse. The eruption could come in a millisecond. If only I knew what would set him off, then I could avoid doing it. I don't know. I often think my mom sets him off on purpose so she can take her ass whipping, get it over with, and move on with her day. She's tough.

I feel helpless as he stands there. I'm a mouse trying to attack the cat. He reaches out to my apron, pink because it was washed with a red shirt. I don't understand. To me, it's just a color. He tugs on my apron and looks at my mom and all the cookies. His eyes get this hollow look. They are soulless. I can see the rage pulsating in my dad's body. The rage and anger seem to seep through every pore. His voice is a low, rumbling roar as he peers into my mom's eyes.

"You're turning him into a little faggot. He's gonna be a gay boy. For god sake, look what you're doing to him."

He draws back his hand and wipes all the cookies to the floor with rage. Then he cocks back his fist to hit my mom. In that moment, my little boy becomes a man. I'm now big and tall. I tower over my dad.

He seems so small, and I feel huge and strong.

"Enough," I say, my voice low, my tone confident.

His fist stops in disbelief, and he gazes at the man I have become. I stare down upon him as his body shrinks to the size of a little boy. He speaks with a timid man's voice in a child's body. Then, finally, he tells the story, a story of abuse and shame.

He tells us a how his uncle would make him strip down to his underwear and put on a pink robe and walk around in women's shoes. He tells us of the shame he felt when his uncle would touch him as if he was a woman. He speaks of the pain he harbored in his heart and soul, the helplessness he felt as an eight-year-old boy. He's been harboring this pain so deep within his soul and tucked away in every cell of his body, and when he recalled moments of his traumatic childhood, that pain would turn to rage. It was dynamite on a volatile fire of emotions that erupted rage on everyone with physical abuse. How was an eight-year-old boy supposed to deal with this much pain?

"How could I ever rid myself of the shame?" He asks, and big tears rumble down his cheeks. It is the first time I've ever seen my dad cry. The pain in his face is deep as he looks to me for answers.

I stand here, a man observing a boy who is my father. He looks up to me and says, "I'm sorry. Please forgive me."

I know he truly means what he's saying but it doesn't magically erase all the years of pain. It is a start, though.

"I can understand why you reacted to situations in life, but that doesn't make it right," I tell him. "I understand the pain you have carried." I have so much more to say and realize all I need to say is, "I forgive you." For the first time in my life, I hug my dad.

Time stands still for moment as peace engulfs the kitchen. My mom grabs a handful of flour and throws it at us. I close my eyes to avoid it, and when I open them, Charlie stands before me and pelts me in the face with snow.

"Look behind you," he says.

I turn to see two KTM motorcycles decked out for deep snow.

Instead of a front tire, there's a ski, and for a rear tire, there's a rubber track that stretches off the back. That track will give the ultimate traction in deep snow. It's as if a snowmobile had merged with a motorcycle and it is faster and better.

"They both have nitrous for that extra push up the mountain," Charlie says and tosses me another pair of oversize goggles. "You might need those. It's game on, West."

I am beyond excited to ride the bike. My adrenaline is pumping as I jump on. I salivate at the smell of two-stroke gas burning. It sounds so good in the middle of nothingness. The bikes are modern-day horses that can't be stopped. They are pure power and beauty that gets my adrenaline surging through my body. I am stoked to ride this bad boy. I look at my boring snowshoes as I twist the throttle and listen to my bike come to life with a roar, braap, braap. Charlie looks at me and revs his engine.

We both nail the throttle, and it's a rush to feel the power of the bike and see the seventy-five-foot rooster tail shooting from the track as we race through the snow. This was truly an awesome display of power and so exhilarating as the front ski floats above the snow. The speed, power, and flow feel so good as I climb the mountain. Charlie and I crisscross each other, and our tracks look like the DNA chain. We are wide fucking open or WFO with no thought of going back. How can I ever go back with this much exhilaration and acceleration propelling me forward? I am in it to win it.

The tree line is fast approaching as the bikes consume ground at a rapid pace. I look for the perfect line to take through the trees and set my sights for an open slot. My sight is interrupted by walls of powder flowing from Charlie's bike. He sprays me with a massive rooster tail of snow and leaves me with no place to go. I ease off the throttle as my visibility becomes zero and I bring my bike to a stop and shake the snow from my body. I pull the over-size googles that Charlie handed me previously over my eyes. I really need that extra layer of protection, and I'm not sure why I didn't put them on earlier. The clarity is amazing as I watch Charlie rip through the trees. He picks the perfect line and is in harmony with his bike.

I gun my throttle wide open, and my bike sputters to a stop. I stand up and put my foot on my kick starter. I try to kick the bike over several times with no success. I put all my weight into it and kick and kicked with no luck. The bike won't start. My breathing escalates as my heart races, and sweat runs off my cheeks. I pull off my goggles, wipe off the sweat, and then put them back on.

I'm startled by the sight of Dawn standing before me. It isn't sweat running down cheeks; it's tears. She stands there with an innocence about her, like something, someone from another lifetime.

One tear rolls from my cheek and floats into the air like a helium balloon. It rises above us, and I can see it has the word "sadness" written on it. The tear of sadness swells above us and hangs in observation before gently washing over the two of us. We each hold our hands out to the side as if the emotion has been cleared from our souls.

Another tear falls from my cheek. This one morphs into a yellowish-orange color and has the word "fear" floating inside. The tear grows and hovers over us before bursting and washing over the two of us. I can feel all the fear being washed away from my body. The sensation is euphoric. I relish in knowing that toxic emotion has been cleansed from me.

A giant red tear falls from my cheek and circles our bodies for what seems like hours. It moves slowly and methodically. Finally. the word "anger" floats in the tear. The word expands and shrinks as it hovers above us. Its neon glow goes from red to orange to white. The glow has an intoxicating effect with a therapeutic pulse. My entire body fixates on the tear as I feel it cleanse me. It's strong and powerful as it washes away my pain. The color changes from red to white as it flows over the two of us. The movement of a simple bubble of light is magical. The tear's pure essence of white light infiltrates every cell of my body. The release of anger sheds itself within seconds, and like that, the bubble is gone. My heart feels healthier. My skin feels cleaner. I can hear and feel my heart beating. The sound is life and it is amazing.

Another tear rolls from my cheek. It is shades of green as it suspends above us with long, stringy pieces of green flowing like kelp. It brushes against us like a young parent bathing an infant. The word "self-destruction" floats within it. The iridescent and the bathing of the kelp-like strings feel so soft to my skin as they cleanse me, and all my self-destructive thoughts seem to float away. I'm liberated of self-destructive soldiers who ran rampant in my body. For the first time in my life, I am in control. I am in control of me. I have been given the opportunity to retrain my army to operate from love. My army is engaged and ready to accept and live in forgiveness.

A light blue tear rolls off my cheek and circles me with enormous speed. The blue light brings comfort like the sky above. The blue light is courage. I am being filled with courage. The courage to feel sadness. The courage to feel pain. The courage to feel fear. The courage to feel anger. The courage to feel self-destruction. The courage to forgive. And ultimately, the courage to give and receive love. The blue light is completely intoxicating as it swirls around my body. The light worked its way to my feet and stays. The feeling is solid and grounding. I have a foundation upon courage to stand on, and nothing can take it away.

A big, pink tear positions itself between Dawn and me. I can see her eyes and face with the tear obscuring my view. The words "accept and forgive" rotated within the pink bubble. The word "accept" comes to my vision first. Acceptance is all I can read, and it's all that I can feel. I truly feel myself accept the divorce. I own it, as if it were my decision. I accept the failure. I accept the embarrassment. I accept my childhood. I accept that my life will be different. The word acceptance goes to Dawn. I can barely see her eyes through the bubble as the word appears backwards to me. There is a peaceful transaction taking place between the two of us, a transaction of well-being.

The word forgiveness presents itself, and I realize this is a big moment. Forgiveness is the key to my letting go. Forgiveness will bring me everlasting happiness. I first forgive myself for all the judgement I harbored. I forgive myself for the resentment. I forgive myself for the jealousy. I forgive myself for the anger. I forgive myself for the sadness. I forgive myself for the lack of communication. I forgive myself for withholding love. I forgive the little boy inside me. It was never his fault. I forgave my dad. Ultimately, I forgive Dawn. I forgive her for asking for a divorce. The word of forgiveness goes to her. I realize in this moment that the energy of marriage has come to an end. The energy put a timestamp on the end of my marriage. The ending is slow and faded like a pair of worn jeans. Jeans feel better over time, but they do wear out eventually, or you grow out of them. It seems to me that marriage really doesn't last forever unless you die together. I silently tell Dawn that I Forgive her. Although my energy feels good, I know I'm not falling in love. I'm falling out of love. I accept this moment, and I forgive myself.

I lift the goggles and find myself standing at the beacon. The air is crisp, and the full moon shines brightly. At the top of the mountain, is a table set for two with one single candle burning brightly. The candle is the beacon of light I've been guided by. It is a simple and elegant place setting. The candle has a bright golden glow with a rainbow circle around it. The rainbow is spectacular. I've never seen anything like it before. The sheer beauty and stillness captivate me. I'm taken in and mesmerized by the light. I've made it to the beacon, and it is far more beautiful than I could have ever imagined.

The quiet of the night is interrupted by Charlie. I haven't noticed him sitting at the table.

"West, have a seat."

I make my way to the table as if I floated there. I feel light but strong and full of life.

"West, I'm proud of you." He stares at me with a loving glow. "Tonight, you will have dinner with the love of your life."

Charlie stands up, reaches for his headlamp, and snaps his

fingers. The headlamp stays the same, and the moon lights up for Charlie. He illuminates the entire mountain in front of him. The light is bright enough to light up a football stadium. He snowboards away, carving with such grace as if he is dancing with the full moon. Pure joy echoes in the trees as he carves a beautiful line down the mountain.

I sit there wondering who will come to dinner. Who will meet me on this amazing mountain top? I am excited fore I know the guidance of Charlie is always spot on.

I'm ready to meet whomever sits across from me and allow myself to give and receive. I feel amazing.

7
LOVE

"Love is the most powerful emotion we can live from"

I sit at the table that is set for two under a moonlit sky. The full moon beams through the cold, crisp mountain air. I should be cold as I sit there in board shorts and a T-shirt. The table setting is quite elegant and simple, an all white table cloth covering the wooden teak table with white dishes. Everything is white except for two small plates. One is orange and at the other place setting, the small plate is green. In the middle of the table where a candle should go is a small and mighty fire pit. The fire is mesmerizing with life. I feel like I could be content staring at this fire for the rest of my life. It exudes pure joy and raw love.

I wonder who will sit across from me. I wonder what we will talk about. My wonderment creates an amazement that leads me to think about what I want in my next relationship. I make a mental checklist for the love I want to receive and share with someone else. I want a beautiful blonde who is fit, active, healthy, loves to surf, laugh, play the guitar, ride motorcycles, and stare at me like I'm a king. Is this too much to ask? No. I know she is out there. I know she will come into my life. I'm ready to attract the person who is ready to attract me.

The trees that surround my mountaintop setting feel like friends. They stretch to the night sky with their branches held out wide. They gently dance in the wind as a gentle hum echoes through the forest. I am sitting in magic. I can feel it. I am part of the magic. I am the magic. The fire dances and sings as I sit contentedly in a state of knowing that I am attracting the most amazing person who will join me.

The flames go high then low. Then they gently sway from side to side, and they do it all without music. All they need is oxygen. The fire is breathing in pure oxygen from the source. A source that surrounds us here, high in the sky. The fire and I share the oxygen as the trees watch in stillness. I want this moment and feeling to last forever without anyone taking it away. I am allowing this moment to happen. I created this moment. I have everything I need to feel the love and pure gratitude for the trees, moon, snow, sky, stars, and air. I am in gratitude.

I reach into the fire with my hand. I want to touch it. I want to hold it. I want it to feel me. It draws me in with her beautiful dance. We truly have become one with each other. It doesn't burn me. She allows my hand to curl around her flames allowing me to be a part of her. I was in awe of its colors, the sounds and movement that need no thoughts or direction. She moved with out thought. She danced without thinking. My focus moves from the fire to the chair that is across from me.

I smile at the eight-year-old boy who sits there and he returns the smile.

"Hi," I say.

"Hi."

"What's your favorite color?" I ask.

"Orange," he says.

"Like the fire?" I ask.

"Yeah," he says. "Like the fire."

"Do you like sitting out here under the stars?"

He says, "I like looking for falling stars and making wishes."

"What do you wish for?" I ask.

"I wish for peace. I wish to laugh. I wish for happiness. I wish for a dad who didn't beat me up. I wish for endless wishes."

"Do you believe in wishes?" I ask him.

"I do now," he says. "I do now."

I stare at him with great admiration and tell him, "I will always fulfill your wishes, and I will always take care of you. I love you."

We smile at each other, and he asks "Can I put my hand in the fire?"

"Yes. You can put both your hands in the fire."

He reaches across the table with both hands stretched out and thrusts them into the fire. His smile is huge, and his laugh is infectious. He tries to grab the flames while laughing and giggling. His laugh comes from deep within his soul, from his heart. He has finally found a safe place to laugh. His laugh is the joy of life. I stare at his hands dancing within the flames. They seem to disappear at times and always in rhythm with the flames. He is in the rhythm of life.

His hands are present before my eyes as I observe the grown

up me sitting across from me. He pulls his hands from the fire, and says, "It's as if the flames are like our soul."

I nod in agreement.

I ask him, "Is this that moment when I talk to myself and feel like I'm talking to someone else?"

"Yes," he says. "Kinda weird, right?"

I look a little different than what I had imagined. I guess if I would have been a twin, this is what it would have felt like. It's a really bizarre feeling. It makes me wonder why parents dress twins the same. What a mind fuck for a three-year-old to look over and see himself.

I ask him, "Would you change anything about your life?"

"No," He answers. "It's made me who I am today."

"I knew you would say that. I'm extremely proud of who you are. You're a warrior. I want you to know that life is for living, life is about emotions. Sometimes we don't want to feel our emotions. You have allowed yourself to feel and process a lifetime of emotions. In order to keep living, you have to feel. In order to live whole, you must allow that emotion to have meaning. Otherwise, life has no meaning. You must allow that emotion to feel. Otherwise, you can't feel. I'm proud of you. I admire you. I accept the person you are. No one can define you. You are the same as the fire. You're dancing in the wind. Love the dance. Love the man you are. Love the emotions you carry. When you live from love, you are living in your highest power. And when you do, you'll sing with the birds, you'll dance like the fire, you'll surf like Kelly Slater, you'll play basketball like Michael Jordan, and you'll throw a pass like Joe Montana. You'll look at a fire with passion and love, and you'll feel the power of the ocean cleanse away the negativity of a day. When you see the world in love, then you know you have arrived. Allow yourself to wake up with gratitude. I love you. I love you. I love you."

I look up from the fire, and he is gone. I know he didn't go far. How could he? He is me. I finally found me. I love the words he spoke. I love the emotions he invoked. I ignored him so many times in my life, but today, I made a pact to always listen to his words and acknowledge his feelings and emotions. I would love what he said and felt whether I liked it or not. I would love me for the rest of my life. I would love.

I look up to the stars and truly feel their presence. I feel that I could reach up and grab a star. I feel a part of the stars.

I gaze at the night sky in full awe and amazement, and vast blanket of nothingness wraps me in love. I know whatever I wish for will come true. I know I was put here for a reason. I was put here to love, no matter what the situation. Maybe I wouldn't always like it. Maybe it would make me feel a little uncomfortable, and if it did, I would love it, no matter what. So that I can truly live and feel life with passion, I have to be okay and accept every crappy, bullshit thing that ever happened to me, and when I put love around that acceptance, I realize that nothing happened to me. It happened for me. I am shining bright like the stars above me.

The real test sits before me. My brightness will be tested as I look across the table at the man who brought me into the world. He sits there emotionless with his dark soul and lifeless body. The little boy inside me fights to shut down and avoid him. The little boy wants nothing to do with this motherfucker. On a physical level, I know I could take him. I could totally kick his ass. He's nothing more than an old man. He's broken. He's been lost his entire life, and when you're so far off your path, you lose your soul.

I really want to pull him into the fire and watch him burn. Why is he here? I wonder and feel my jaw clinch tightly shut and my muscles tense. I hear and feel the memory of grinding my teeth as a boy. The sound is haunting. It resonates through every cell in my body. I had been at war with this motherfucker I called, dad for my entire life. What a piece of shit. It was a war of physical and mental abuse. I had witnessed beat downs on my mom and people I didn't even know, and here I sit across from him with my fists tightly clinched and my cells rock hard.

He stretches his hands across the table. His fists are bigger than normal. They are massive, and they have words tattooed on them. The words are in big, black letters. I read, SADNESS. He holds his hands in the fire as the flames danced around the letters.

"Today, I'm going to tell you a story," he says. "The story won't erase my behavior, but I hope it brings you peace." He peers at his hands in the fire for a moment. "The word represents a baby who was born into a world with a sister and two brothers. I was the last child to be born from a mother who died shortly after giving birth. I carried the blame, grief, and utter sadness from and for my father. And just like my father, I was unable to communicate my feelings. He blamed me for the loss of his wife, my mom, your grandmother. She died, and I was the pincushion for emotional and physical abuse. That pincushion was stuck every time my dad felt sad or lonely or angry. I was left with neighbors, relatives, and an orphanage. I was left with whoever would take me. No mom. No love."

I listen to his story and watch as the letters of sadness drips from his hands. His hands slowly roll in the fire, and another word comes up, also in big, black letters, ANGER. Then RAGE. The flames dance around the letters. The words are defiant. The fire doesn't seem to affect them. They don't budge.

The intensity of the fire increases and focuses on the first letter of each word. The A in anger begins to crackle and pop, slowly disappearing. The cracking and popping continue while my dad tells another story.

"At the age of fourteen, I went to work at an all-girls summer camp. The camp had horses and a clear blue lake for swimming and canoeing. My brothers would teach the girls to ride horses, swim, canoe and go hiking. The camp was all about instilling confidence. I was in awe of my brothers. I wanted to be like them, and one day changed my life forever. In that one day, I was injected with more fear, anger, and terror. I was called to the barn by the man who ran the camp. He told me he would give me love. I desperately wanted to be loved. The man was a beast. He violated my trust as he gave me a hug that felt warm and inviting. I wanted to feel love. I didn't know what it felt like. The beast of a man took advantage of a little boy. He violated my body. He did things to me that are inconceivable. I could never get past the disgust. I couldn't and wouldn't talk about it. I ate my anger everyday. Every single day, I ate so much anger. I ate it with a vengeance. And then I would have days that I needed to store my anger else where. I spewed it anywhere I could. I spewed my rage. I spewed on you and your mom. I spewed on people I didn't know. And the only way I could make it go away was with drugs and alcohol. I self-medicated myself like no one else. I put a steel blanket over my haunting memories and never told a soul. I would stuff my body with drugs for the rest of my life so I didn't have to relive the pain, guilt, fear, grief, disgust, anger, and rage. I didn't realize we were all living it. You never understood why the volcano would erupt, and I never knew when it was going to happen, and I didn't know why. I was trying to survive. I wanted to live, but I didn't know how. I wanted to love, but I didn't know how. I figured out how to die and kill everything I loved."

I watch as the letters fade from his hands, losing their battle to the fire of life. The flames consume the words. They are gone.

He rolls his hands in the fire, and the word, ACCEPTANCE appears. He looks at me with a gentler soul exuding from his eyes.

"I'm sorry."

I hear his words and utter, "I forgive you." I reach into the fire and hold his hands. "I forgive you." And with the uttering of those three words, his acceptance tattoo fades away and FORGIVENESS appears.

The tension I hold in my muscles begins to loosen. My jaw feels free. My soul feels free. I look at this man who is and will always be my father. A man who I've been embarrassed to call Dad. The man I wanted to kill.

I look at him and say, "What you have lived, I have lived. I love you, dad. I will love you forever."

I hold his hand in the fire. The word LOVE appears one letter at a time on his hand. He is tattooed with LOVE.

He holds my hand tightly, and with a soft, gentle voice says, "I love you, son and I'm proud of you. You broke the chain. You broke the chain."

And with those last words, he is gone.

I sit in gratitude for what I've learned. I've learned to love from his lack of love. I've learned to trust from his lack of trust. I've learned to live from his inability to live. In the end, he had love his entire life and didn't know it.

I've faced him and didn't shut down. I faced sadness, fear, anger, self-destruction, courage, forgiveness, and love. Thank you, Dad, I think, for showing me the way. I guess this map of life was a little different than most. Thank you.

I sit there wondering what life would have been like if I could have had this conversation with my dad years ago. What would life have been like if he would have sought help? I could ask these questions all day long, but it really doesn't matter. I am who I am, and I am who I want to be.

I sit back in my chair and witness the biggest, brightest shooting star I've ever seen race across the sky. The clarity of my vision is so clear that I could see it with my eyes closed. The star's trail leaves a hint of color as it dances across the sky. I make my wish and I know it will come true. I can see my wish with my eyes closed. My eyes are looking at my soul. I can feel my wish. In this moment, I feel so alive and full of love that I know I am in alignment with the universe. I can see it, and I don't need to put words to a picture that I can feel. Words wouldn't do it justice. Words would muck it up. I know my wish would be present when the hair on my neck stands up. I know I will feel it when the pit of my stomach dances with fire. I know I will feel it when my sentences become silly, laughable words. I am open to receiving. I am open to feeling. I am open 24/7. I am alive, and I am ready.

Dawn appears in the chair across from me. My 24/7 open sign seems to blow in the wind. Am I really open? Am I really ready? She sits there, ready to talk. Am I ready to listen? I want to blame. I want to shut down. I want to scream at her, go fuck yourself. I sit for a moment, thinking about time before marriage when we shared the silence and beauty of watching a sunset. It was a great time then, no worries, no stress. Life was simple. Life was easier. We wanted to get married then. We wanted to have children. I never thought would it last or not last. I didn't know. Looking back now, I realize it was a part of my journey. I had to take the journey to get to this point in my life. I look across the fire at her, but she is gone, nothing more than a few embers.

She looks at me and says. "I forgive you."

Did she just say she forgives me? I have to really think about that. She's forgiving me? She asks for the divorce, and now she is forgiving me. My first thought is, Fuck You. That's not the answer I was looking for. If I shout, "Fuck you," that would slow my journey down. Fuck you would be a big negative roadblock.

I have to ask her, "Why do you forgive me?"

She says, "I forgive you for shutting down."

I realize then what I had been taught. I was the opposite force from my father's rage. I was the opposite force from my father's anger and sadness. Through her forgiveness, I accept my short-comings.

"I'm sorry," I tell her. "I'm sorry we couldn't work it out."

I stare at the coals that struggle to find oxygen. They are a clear representation of our relationship. Our oxygen is gone. It's not in my nature to quit. I truly believe I can keep a fire going in the rain. She is the girl with the power and strength to end it and move on. The energy tied with emotions is strong. It's like undoing welds on metal. When you grind away the weld, you leave a mark or a scar. I guess that scar is there to remind you what you did wrong. I am keeping my scars to remind me of what I did right. We're both amazing people who lost their way. We both came to the table with baggage. We came along way to finally sit down at the table without casting blame or shame. We are the same but different. I accept divorce. I accept the blame. I accept the shame. I accept myself.

I look at her and say, "I forgive you, and I forgive me, and I forgive us." We hold hands one last time over the coals as they spell out FRIENDSHIP. And just like that, twenty years of marriage disappears. We still have the byproduct of two amazing and beautiful children.

I let a tear roll off my cheek. It is over, and the truth is, it was over a long time ago. I had held on for the little boy inside me who desperately wanted a normal family.

Twenty years flew by in a flash. Twenty years can be an excruciating amount of time. My twenty years had been filled with love combined with numb and excruciating silence. The woman across from me asked for a divorce more than two years ago. These two years have felt like fifty years. I've never felt so much sadness. I've never felt so much fear. I've never felt so much anger. I've never felt so dead inside. I truly wanted to die. And in that time, I found other emotions that I hadn't felt in a long time. I've never felt so much courage. I've never felt so much forgiveness. I've never felt so much love.

I didn't know it at the time that I had to go deep inside myself to allow love back in my life. I was open to receive love. The fire roared back to life. I sat there fulfilled by my journey. I was proud of myself. I felt whole and complete. I felt so good inside. My heart was full and I was entirely by myself. I wondered if I was complete. What does it mean to be complete in life? How could you ever feel happy if you never felt sorrow? I was happy. I knew in my heart that I wanted and would allow myself to love. I wanted to surround myself in love. I wanted to live in love. What I learned through this journey is that love is the greatest emotion we can operate from. Love carries the ultimate reservoir of strength. From this day forward, love would be the driving force behind my thoughts and actions. I was going to live in love. I could see it. I could feel it. I could taste it. There was no need to explain it. Love is not a word, it's an emotion.

There was a tap on my shoulder, and Bob Marley stood by my side and said, "Love the life you live and live the life you love." He gave me a Shaka and faded away. In that moment, I chose to live everyday in love. I know I'll feel sadness, fear and anger and when I do, love will get me through it.

I stood up in my chair, and looked to the stars, holding my hands out wide. I was ready to receive love. I waited for the lightning bolt. I waited for the ray of light. I stood in total stillness. Nothing. I had my eyes closed and was ready to receive. My silence was broken by the loudest fart ever. Charlie stood beside me, laughing and giggling like a kid. I couldn't help but giggle too.

He said, "A loud fart will always bring laughter." He put his arm around me, and added, "I have an idea. I truly believe it's one of my greatest ideas ever." He waved his hand in a 360-degree circle around us. "I present to you, the Moat."

We were suddenly ringed by a fire. This beautiful fire danced in the night and made me feel secure.

Charlie said, "Look, you have the fire on the table for your hands and heart, and a ring of fire that has your back. Everyone needs someone to have their back."

As simple as it seemed, Charlie brought a fire moat to life. I couldn't help but hear Johnny Cash singing, Ring Of Fire.

Charlie said, "Johnny Cash is a legend, but this night deserves the rock of AC/DC." The song You Shook Me All Night Long blasted full blast in the quiet of the night. The music moved my soul. The music moved my feet. The fire gave it life. The fire roared with such intensity as I danced with the Borealis lights. The lights kept beat with the music and so did the fire. This was rock n' roll heaven. I had arrived. Could life get any better? I wanted to live here forever. I want to spend the rest of my life protected by the moat. I was safe. I could dance. I could sing. I was in my own world. Nothing could penetrate the moat. The fire would grow with intensity as my body screamed with exuberance.

I screamed out, "I am open to happiness." I held my hands out wide and opened my heart to the night sky. "I am open to receive happiness."

I could feel the amazing energy I was surrounded in. I was alive again. I was dancing without realizing I was dancing. I didn't think about dancing. I danced. My bliss felt so good, I could touch it. How could I be so lucky? My body spewed with gratitude. The more gratitude I felt, the larger the fire roared. I twirled in circles as my feet stomped to the beat of AC/DC. I held my hands out wide to receive all the greatness I had cut off from my life. I was living. My life felt complete. Here I was, dancing under a starlit sky on a mountaintop with a raging fire and rock n' roll blasting. I watched hundreds of shooting stars race across the night sky. I was pumping with gratitude. I was pumping with joy. I was pumping with love. It was time to make a wish. The night sky was lit up with tracers beaming across the blackness. I had arrived and I was only one song into my journey. I didn't need a map. I had a vision. I had dreams. I had passion. I had bliss. I was living in bliss. I laid my arms out wide, with my head tilted toward the sky, and I pulled words deep from inside. I screamed as loud as I could, "I am open to receive love, I am open to give love." The music stopped and all I could see was my breath.

The ring of fire went to nothing. The fire on the table danced with beauty. The intensity of the full moon shined upon me. It truly was the largest full moon I had ever seen in my life. I was drawn in by the size, beauty, and unbelievable moon bow that circled it. The moon bow circled the entire moon in an orange-and-green ring. The two colors blended so beautifully together as if they had always been together. I was in gratitude to see such a spectacular display of beautiful light.

I turned to the table to see a beautiful woman sitting with flowing blond hair lit by the moon. Her green eyes radiated love, happiness, and joy. Her beautiful smile and white teeth captured my attention as our gazes locked onto each other.

"I'm Best," I said, "I mean West." How could I not stumble saying my name. Her beauty and aura captured mine.

She said with her soft voice, "I'm Suzie."

I looked to the moon and winked while whispering, "Thank you."

Suzie sat there looking so angelic. I kept asking myself, how could I be so lucky. I knew it wasn't luck. I made a wish for a beautiful woman. I visualized this woman coming into my life. I allowed it to happen.

"Do you surf?" I ask her.

"Yes," She said, and I was ecstatic inside.

"Do you ride motorcycles?"

"Yes." Oh my god, I thought. I think I found the perfect woman. And then she said, "I like fast cars. My favorite is a Porsche, and I play the guitar."

The fire around the moat rose higher and higher as we learned that we had so much in common.

"Do you believe in eating dessert first?" I asked.

"As long as we can share it."

I pointed to the moon. "Look at the moon bow."

"Green is my favorite color," she said. "What's yours?"

"Mine is orange."

This moment could not have been more perfect. Our emotions were so in alignment, and everything felt so easy as if we had known each other for years. Our energy collided as the moon's ray pulled us onto the table. The table expanded to provide a place to dance. We came together and embraced. The moment was magical and filled with gratitude. I asked if she was real, and she ask me the same. The ring of fire around us provided a safe place for our emotions to merge, and the starlit sky let us know anything was possible. The song Dancing In The Moonlight by King Harvest began playing. I pulled her in tight, and our bodies swayed as if they were one. We truly had merged into one being. Our souls had collided, and we had each other's backs. The moment was deep. The moment was rich. The moment was simple.

Our bodies were in sync with every beat. I loved how she felt. I loved how she smelled. We allowed the music to move our bodies. We allowed the music to move our souls. We didn't need each other to dance. We could dance by ourselves. We wanted to dance together. We became a stronger team together. The fire danced with us. The stars danced with us. The trees danced with us. We all became one with one another and danced with love and gratitude. I would remember our magical night forever. It felt good to let go and be at one with Suzie. It felt better than good, It felt amazing. The dance was bliss. The dance was movement. The dance was electrifying. There we were on the table, holding each other tightly under the spell of the moon light. This was the highest of highs.

The song came to an end, but our energy had given birth to a new relationship that felt so bonded and grounded within the ring of fire. I had spent years putting up a cold, hard wall around myself, and if you were on the outside, you didn't get in. If you were on the inside, you froze to death. Tonight, my wall was a raging fire filled with love. Our souls lit this fire with a volcanic eruption that poured our feelings onto the table. We were able to give and receive love. A new life had emerged from the fire, and we were going to sing a new song together. We were going to sing, laugh, surf, and love till the day we died. I was filled with so much gratitude for this beautiful woman. I felt her gratitude for me. I felt her love for me.

We stared into each other's eyes. The silence had no timestamp. I didn't know if it had been ten seconds or ten years. Words would never be able to describe the emotions that we felt. We didn't need words. We felt it, we knew it.

I said to her, "Remember this moment, so we can relish in it twenty two years from now."

The silence was broken by the sound of a black helicopter. It dropped from above with two lines dangling from its skids. I couldn't see the pilot, and I really didn't need to see the pilot. I trusted Charlie and knew it was him.

We grabbed the lines without hesitation, and away we lifted. We each pulled ourselves into the body of the chopper as the wind blew her beautiful blond hair. She looked like a goddess climbing the rope, and I felt like a warrior. I gave one last look below at the beautiful setting on the mountain. The ring of fire blazed as I felt the beauty of the night. My thoughts of allowing this beautiful woman into my life were greater than I could have ever imagined. I had burned my walls down and let someone into my life who was simply amazing. I could taste the freedom in the air and knew that from this day forward, life would be an adventure. I was going to live a great life and trusted that wherever this helicopter was taking us would be amazing. I trusted the pilot even though I didn't know who it was. I trusted the moment. I trusted this beautiful woman who sat next to me.

The sun rose as we crested over the top of the mountain peak. I could feel the golden sun on my face. I could see the sun and feel its rays just like the ring of fire. I could see the golden sun radiating around the beauty of this amazing beautiful blond woman.

Charlie's voice came over the intercom.

"Good morning, West and Suzie, and welcome to the most magical place in the world. West, you will find a new orange snowboard, just as I promised, and Suz, I have a magical green board for you. Today, you will have first tracks for as long as you can go."

We jumped out of the chopper and stood in the snow with our boards and watched Charlie disappear.

Suzie pointed into the blue metallic sky and drew a perfect rainbow with her index finger. I had provided a moat of fire, and she drew a rainbow. The moment was stunning and magical.

We blasted our way down the mountain, me on my orange snowboard and Suzie on her green one. We threw huge carves with walls of snow going fifty feet in the air. Our carves were epic, effortless, and in sync with one another. We didn't think about where we were going. We stayed in the flow. Our turns seem to last forever. The moment was euphoric. It almost felt orgasmic. How could we make turns that could last so long and throw huge walls of snow that hung in the air for eternity or what felt like eternity? We shared this moment together. We shared this mountain together. We were one with the mountain. We didn't speak with words, but with energy. Our energy collided as our bodies flowed down the mountain on frozen particles of water. The snow felt soft like cotton, and our tracks seemed to merge as we crisscrossed one another. My soul felt so grounded and at peace with myself and the world around me. The rainbow Suzie drew stretched above us with vivid colors and followed us down the mountain. The rainbow began to flatten as we approached its colorful arch.

I turned to Suzie and said, "When you know, you know."

The arch collapsed upon us, and the visibility went to zero. We were in the rainbow. I couldn't see her, and she couldn't see me. And in a flash, I popped out to blue sky.

The girl of my dreams was gone, and I was sitting on my surfboard, waiting for a wave. I wanted to see her paddle up next to me. I wanted to see her beautiful smile. I wanted to see her strong legs. I knew she was still a part of me without physically seeing her. I had to trust that I would see her again. I could see her in my mind. I felt gratitude for Suzie. I looked out to the horizon and saw the wave of my life rolling toward me. There was no one out but me. This was my wave.

I turned and took three strokes and popped to my feet. I caught the wave so easily. I dropped into a gentle giant that allowed me to get the barrel of my life. I could hear the swoosh of water coming over the top of my head and feel the power of the ocean propelling me across her face. The view out the curl was spectacular. The view was amazing. Time stood still inside the silence of my mind as I moved effortlessly. I reached my hand out to her face and gently touched it. She was beautiful. She was powerful. She was graceful. I knew that at any moment, Mother Nature could take it away from me. I'd be grateful either way. I was merely along for the ride. The foam ball chased me from behind, and all at once, her mighty lip collapsed just as she spat me out of her mighty grip. I squeaked out the curtain of water into the real world.

My dream had come to an end.

I cupped handfuls of water and splashed myself in the face as I stood at the sink in my grandmother's hospital bathroom. My hair looked crazy and disheveled as if I had been camping for months.

I felt grounded. I felt whole. I felt more alive than I ever had. I felt happy. I walked out of the bathroom to be with my grandmother. She was resting peacefully in bed and she radiated beauty. She appeared to be sleeping as I approached her bed.

Her eyes opened and without hesitation she asked, "Did you meet Charlie?" I nodded my head yes with a smile.

She looked at me with that proud grandmother look. She had the glow of knowing all that I had dreamed. She spoke with love and purity. "I have someone I want you to meet." She pushed the call button on her remote to summon a nurse.

A beautiful woman entered the room. She wore a baseball cap, and her blond hair was pulled into a ponytail. Her eyes were hidden by the brim of the hat and I couldn't tell if she was a nurse or someone coming into the wrong room. However, she did walk in with confidence.

"West," my grandmother said. "This is Suzie. She's a physical therapist here, and I kinda felt like you two should meet."

The woman of my dreams stood before me. I wondered if she knew that and wondered if she remembered being part of those dreams. Our gazes locked, and I felt our souls connect. I reached for her hand with mine and we shook hands.

"I know you," she said. "I mean I know who you are. Your grandmother has told me a lot about you."

I heard her voice for the first time, and magic came from her lips. She was beautiful. Her voice was beautiful. And I knew I must appear as if I'd been on a camping trip for weeks.

I pointed to my hair. "I usually look a little better than this." It felt so corny to say that, but I didn't know how else to begin.

"I love how you slept on the floor and kept watch over your grandmother." Suzie said.

My grandmother chimed in, "Charlie was here too."

I looked at Suzie and asked, "Would you like to get a coffee sometime?" "I'd love to." She reached out and touched my shoulder. "And I would love to surf with you."

I watched her walk out of the room and then turned to my grandmother and hugged her.

She whispered in my ear, "Love the life you live, live the life you love. Bob Marley said that."

"I know"

My grandmother held me tight and said, "By the way, Suzie rides a motorcycle to work."

"I'm on it," I told her as we hugged. "I'm on it, Grandma. Life is good."

The beginning...

ASK CHARLIE
NOTES